Selected Fables

JEAN DE LA FONTAINE

Selected Fables

Translated with an Introduction and Notes by

CHRISTOPHER BETTS

OXFORD
UNIVERSITY PRESS

OXFORD
UNIVERSITY PRESS

Great Clarendon Street, Oxford OX2 6DP
United Kingdom

Oxford University Press is a department of the University of Oxford.
It furthers the University's objective of excellence in research, scholarship,
and education by publishing worldwide. Oxford is a registered trade mark of
Oxford University Press in the UK and in certain other countries

© Christopher Betts 2014

The moral rights of the author have been asserted

First published 2014

Impression: 1

Published in the United States of America by Oxford University Press
198 Madison Avenue, New York, NY 10016, United States of America

British Library Cataloguing in Publication Data
Data available

Library of Congress Control Number: 2013948403

ISBN 978–0–19–965072–9

Printed by
Clays Ltd, St Ives plc

CONTENTS

❦

THE EARLY FABLES
(BOOKS I TO VI, 1668)

THE LATER FABLES

(BOOKS VII TO XI, 1677–8, AND BOOK XII, 1693)

LIST OF ILLUSTRATIONS

INTRODUCTION

✌︎

At La Fontaine's birth in 1621 nothing suggested that, as the first son of a well-off provincial family, with no known literary talents or connections, he would even become a writer, let alone a great poet; and it took a long time. In the normal way of things, he would have continued to live as his father had in Château-Thierry north-east of Paris, carrying out his duties as *maître des eaux et forêts*, a supervisor of the region's woods and waterways—an important post in the almost wholly rural France of the seventeenth century—while adding to the family fortunes by dealing in and managing property. But the poetic gift was there, and developed, in which process the parental resources helped: he did not have to earn a living. Gradually everything but the poetry became unimportant. He dissipated the family money, becoming dependent on the generosity of wealthy friends and patrons. In business, although he followed in his father's administrative footsteps for years, he gradually abandoned his duties and lost the income they brought. He married when a marriage was arranged for him, and some five years later, Marie Héricart being fourteen when they married, he fathered a son, their only child, whom he seems to have completely neglected; on one occasion, having met him at some social gathering, he is said not to have recognized him.

Naturally easy-going, La Fontaine must also have been blessed with great personal charm, since besides numerous love-affairs, mostly untraceable, he made and kept a wide range of friends, several of whom were patrons also. The best friend, and the first (they may have met while still at school), was François de Maucroix, a poet too, who became a priest and was to be a lifelong confidant. The marriage, despite the affairs, possibly on both sides, seems also to have settled down to a relationship of friendship. Perhaps literature helped; Marie was a relative of Racine, who also became one of La Fontaine's friends and corresponded with Marie about literary matters. Family in the wider sense still counted. An uncle of Marie's, Jannart, a lawyer and experienced man of business, seems to have kept an eye on the financial affairs of both of them, accommodated them in Paris on their visits from Château-Thierry, and helped at the outset of La Fontaine's literary career. And despite poetic absentmindedness, for in company he could be completely silent at times, or else determined to hold forth on some author he was currently obsessed with, he was popular at all levels of society, from student literary gatherings to the elegant salons kept by ladies of the aristocracy.

In due course poetic ambition drew La Fontaine permanently to Paris, for the public available in a small provincial town was negligible, although his wife is believed to have presided over a literary society at home. Besides the usual temptations of a capital, to which he seems happily to have yielded, the city held other writers whose stimulus was essential, it had well-stocked libraries, and offered opportunities for publishing and patronage. But writing seems to have become his dominant preoccupation only after a false start with religion. His stay at the Oratoire in 1641–2 implies that he must have been seriously attracted by the religious life, like his brother and Maucroix, since he sampled it for over a year, but then he gave up and went home. Even so, numerous later poems and translations of religious texts show that the religious impulse was not merely transitory.

Whatever the precise course of his poetic development, after a few years in Château-Thierry and legal studies in Paris he was a versifier proficient enough to join with other young men in the literary society they called the Round Table, 'La Table ronde': perhaps the name of a tavern where they met. The law qualification was supposed to help with family business and the official post that his father, no doubt, had already planned for him. He did fulfil his duties as *maître des eaux et forêts* for a while—even for an impractical poet, they appear not to have been demanding—but his time gradually became divided between Château-Thierry and Paris. The definitive break seems to have come with the death of his father in 1658 and his roughly contemporaneous entry into the magic world of Fouquet's circle, where his position was a semi-public confirmation of his status as poet. It was now that he found appreciation for his poetry from people who really mattered in the literary world, such as Mme de Sévigné or Molière, as opposed to student contemporaries or provincial admirers, and it must have been from that time that the demands of the Muse were reinforced by the sense that his social position depended on writing.

Nicolas Fouquet, officially finance minister but a virtual head of government, hugely wealthy, a charismatic and generous figure, was the ideal patron, sponsoring all the arts in his residences at Vaux-le-Vicomte and Saint-Mandé. Most of what has survived of La Fontaine's verse from this time eulogizes the beauties of Vaux; another poem for Fouquet was *Adonis*, a treatment of the Greek myth following Ovid, and there is no reason to doubt the genuineness of the admiring gratitude that La Fontaine expressed in his dedication. The abrupt and brutal removal of Fouquet by the young Louis XIV, bent on showing that he alone would govern, and jealous of self-aggrandizement in a mere subject, was a huge blow to La Fontaine, as to many others in Fouquet's entourage, among them Jannart. Both remained loyal, despite the risks of royal disfavour. Jannart was temporarily banished—a standard sanction—to distant Limoges, and La Fontaine accompanied him on the journey, probably of his own volition. The letters he wrote on the way, addressed to his wife, contain some moving passages about seeing one of the fortresses in which Fouquet had been imprisoned while awaiting trial. La Fontaine did for him what he could, by publishing anonymously poems in his defence and pleading for clemency. The effects of his attachment to Fouquet are the most controversial subject in his career: did the ever-suspicious Louis XIV hold it against him? Some later events suggest that he did, others not. Did La Fontaine, for his part, continue to resent the king's conduct?[1] Passages in his work that are overtly about the king suggest complete loyalty, but the king-figure in the *Fables*, namely the lion, is seldom portrayed favourably; the court even less so.

With a ready-made, distinguished, but restricted public dispersed, La Fontaine had to find, or be helped to find, another patron. The dowager duchess of Orléans was of the highest rank, but perhaps fortunately took no interest in the literary activities of her secretarial assistant. He became an author, and a prolific one at that. Henceforth his works, even if circulated privately beforehand, would be paid for

---

[1] The tension between poet and king is the subject of a major work by Fumaroli (see Select Bibliography).

by publishers and were intended for the reading public. His first great success was the *Contes*, mischievous tales about seduction, adultery, and sexual deception. No claim to moral edification here; the stories are wholly for entertainment. Some wrongdoers suffer condign punishment, but generally the tone is of amused tolerance, with occasional words of advice for lovers and dupes. Hardly had the third collection of *Contes* appeared than, in 1668, he published the first collection of the *Fables*. They resemble the tales in being verse narratives on borrowed subjects, but are otherwise totally different, and almost look like a bid for respectability. They were dedicated to the six-year-old dauphin, which could not have been managed without permission, at least tacit, from the king. The volume included an entertaining and completely fictitious Life of Aesop, and had a long preface arguing, in support of the dedication, that the fables had great educational value. This seems doubtful, given their subtlety, but French schoolchildren ever since have learned them.

Shaping the Fable

How La Fontaine settled on the fable form has been much debated. It was normal to imitate 'the ancients', from Homer onwards; one of La Fontaine's favourite poets, Horace, had sometimes included fables in his works, for instance 'The Town Rat and the Country Rat'. He knew the prose Aesop, or the fables which went under his name, at school: it was a standard exercise for boys to rewrite them in their own words. Innumerable editions were available, often including lengthy moral reflections. From one by Le Maître de Sacy, a Jansenist, La Fontaine took some ideas for his preface. The first collection of Aesopic fables in Latin verse, written by Phaedrus in the first century AD, was published only in 1596; most of the early fables by La Fontaine which have been preserved in manuscripts owe much to him.[2] There had also been Aesopic collections, in the previous century, in French verse, which La Fontaine certainly knew at some time.

---

[2] See Philip Wadsworth, *Young La Fontaine: A Study of his Artistic Growth in his Early Poetry and First Fables* (Evanston, Illinois: Northwestern University Press, 1952), especially 178–88 on the importance of Phaedrus.

Although the first fable of Book III may perhaps date from earlier,[3] the probability is that La Fontaine began serious work on the Fables only in the 1660s, and no doubt especially after the *Contes* were published. There survives also an unpublished fable, not from Aesop, *Le Renard et l'Ecureuil* ('The Fox and the Squirrel'). It must concern Fouquet (whose name in Old French meant 'squirrel') and his enemy Colbert; it was perhaps written about 1661, soon after Fouquet's imprisonment. It exemplifies a different, but longstanding, use for the fable form: it had often been turned to political purposes, allegorizing persons and situations of contemporary importance. La Fontaine wrote a number of this type, but published only those with some lasting significance.[4] Two in the 1668 collection, I.12 and 13, make general points about statecraft, that command is more effective when united than when divided, and that small states are all too vulnerable to predatory raids by powerful neighbours. The later collection was bolder, for instance with a much more elaborate poem, 'The Power of Fables' (VIII.4). It discusses the looming threat to France from the Protestant powers, and claims that a fable may succeed in gaining attention where ordinary rhetoric does not.

Within the convention of imitation, La Fontaine's originality lay partly in the choice of genre, and partly in the choice of treatment; his was the *fable ornée*, 'ornamented' as opposed to plain, and of course in verse. A respected literary figure whom La Fontaine knew, the lawyer Olivier Patru, had circulated three Aesopic fables of his own; they were in prose and short, illustrating what he believed to be the essential brevity of a fable. In his preface, La Fontaine respectfully disagrees. He brings to his defence no less an authority than Socrates, who facing death put fables into verse as a distraction, and remarks disingenuously that extreme brevity is beyond his abilities (while hinting at disapproval for it in the prologue to VI.1). He himself, he says, has tried to *égayer*, enliven, his fables, and, since the stories are so well known, to renew their interest by what he calls vaguely 'some

[3] See the general note to this fable.

[4] He left unpublished his adaptation of a contemporary political fable in Latin (*Sol et ranae*, 'The Sun and the Frogs'), by the Jesuit Father Commire writing against Holland in about 1671; the sun is Louis XIV, the frogs are the Dutch, considered to live in marshes.

other little touches'. As for *gaieté*, it is 'a certain charm, an attractive air that can be given to all kinds of subjects, even the most serious'. No examples, but the early pair of fables on death (I.15 and 16) would suit. In the first, the man's abrupt change of heart when he comes face to face with Death has its humorous side, and in a note inserted before the second La Fontaine explains that it has been added because otherwise he would have omitted one of Aesop's 'best touches' (*traits*, the word used in the Preface), which must be the woodcutter's similar but more amusing change of heart in the same circumstances.

The Later Years and the Second Collection of Fables

The success La Fontaine enjoyed with the tales and the fables had confirmed his reputation by 1670, late enough. Then came changes, as always; variousness, he said in a much-quoted remark, was his motto: 'Diversité c'est ma devise' (from a *conte*, *Pâté d'Anguille*, 'Eel Pâté', where he means love-affairs rather than writing). He undertook a completely different type of narrative in the mythological novel *Psyché*, a romance in prose, some of the most elegant ever written, but with some passages in verse (it was easier, he explained). The work was to be the basis of a popular opera, not by La Fontaine, but did not itself receive as much acclaim as his verse collections, and the experiment was not repeated. With the death of the duchess of Orléans in 1672 a new period began: he came under the patronage of Mme de La Sablière. He had known her husband many years earlier; the couple now lived apart. She was an intellectual and writer who kept a modest but distinguished salon attended by many more or less free-thinking personalities. Her influence on La Fontaine was as great as Fouquet's and lasted longer. 'Iris' he calls her in dedications; he almost certainly loved her, although she was herself devoted to a man-about-town and minor poet, the Marquis de La Fare. She was however pious, and may have reawakened the latent religious streak in her protégé, for in 1673 came a poem about a saint's resistance to the temptations of the flesh, *De la captivité de Saint-Malc* (the obscure St Malchus), another of the one-off types of production that intersperse his career.

By way of contrast, again, he published more, and bawdier, tales in 1674. These *Nouveaux Contes* were banned as being too audacious, all relating the misdeeds of members of the clergy. In the same year, Boileau published the magisterial *Art poétique*. It has much to say about the genres of poetry, but nothing about fables, even though Boileau had himself inserted a fable in an earlier work. This, no doubt intentionally, illustrates the unadorned type of fable rejected by La Fontaine, who not long after, in 1677–8, published his second large collection of fables, together with all those published in 1668. It was in effect a repudiation of Boileau's dismissive attitude: the fable in its 'adorned' form could claim to be literature.

The new collection was dedicated to a figure of great influence, the then *maîtresse en titre* of Louis XIV, Mme de Montespan, whom the poet entreats to protect his work, successfully it would seem. The brief preface makes no pretence that the fables have educational value for children: this is more clearly a collection for adults. The stories are still taken largely from ancient sources, but the net is cast wider, to include tales from the Orient, and the tone is often more personal and philosophical. Through Mme de La Sablière and her salon, La Fontaine had become acquainted with intellectuals of a kind he had not mixed with before, including scientists, but particularly the doctor, traveller, and orientalist François Bernier, to whom she also extended her patronage. It was very probably he who called La Fontaine's attention to another tradition of fable-writing than the Aesopic: that found in the Sanskrit *Pañcatantra*, often attributed to Bidpai or Pilpay. The exotic type of narrative found there became an important source for the later fables, 'The Metamorphosis of the Mouse' (IX.7) and 'The Two Adventurers and the Talisman' (X.13), for example. However, La Fontaine preserves his habit of keeping the fables separate from one another, whereas in the *Pañcatantra* and other Eastern collections they are linked together, illustrating points made didactically in the frame story. The personal turn that La Fontaine often gave them is perhaps best seen in 'The Two Doves' (IX.2), with its famous epilogue on love, or 'The Dream of One who Lived in Mogul Lands' (XI.4), taken from the Persian poet Saadi, ending with lines on the delights of solitude. The reflections in these later books are often weightier and more ambitious than before, as in 'The Danube Peasant' (XI.7), a political fable protesting against the greed of colonizing governments.

Bernier was also an opponent of the newly-dominant philosopher Descartes, having written a popularization of his less eminent rival, Gassendi. One issue separating them was particularly relevant to a writer of animal tales, the problem known as 'l'âme des bêtes', the soul of beasts. Descartes denied that animals had souls, or could think: for him they worked by instinct, and were in effect mechanical automata. His argument was clearly much in La Fontaine's mind when writing the later fables, and several speak strongly against it. The ninth book concludes with a lengthy *Discours* on the subject, addressed to Mme de La Sablière (from which I give only one short extract here); another late fable, the only one in which he himself has an active role (X.14), extends the argument to show how human behaviour reflects that of animals.

In 1680 Mme de La Sablière was abandoned by La Fare; while continuing to provide for her house poet, piety and the care of the sick became her chief concern. Perhaps this change in her interests had something to do with the appearance of one of La Fontaine's most unexpected long poems, the *Poème du Quinquina* (1682), on the healing properties of quinine, a recent discovery. However, his association with her was weakened. He mixed with less reputable friends, the freethinking and free-living 'société du Temple', the residence of the Vendôme brothers, of royal blood but ostentatiously recalcitrant to the mood of pious gloom that settled over the Court. He had been tempted for a time to join the well-established and sophisticated French community in London, also freethinking, some of whom he knew well. Nothing came of it: Paris retained its charms. Some new fables appeared: ten in 1685, in a publication containing works by Maucroix, which no doubt would not have sold well otherwise. With a scattering of others, they later went to make up the twelfth book. At the same time he continued to write for the stage, still, despite his eminence in verse, with no success: a play in 1683, a tragic opera in 1691.

La Fontaine was now a public figure, but even so much remains obscure. It is not known exactly why the king held back his election to the Académie Française: perhaps because of the disreputable *Contes*, perhaps because of his association with Fouquet, who by then had died in prison. The poet became an assiduous academician, working particularly on its long-delayed dictionary, but whatever the king thought about him he did not prevent some of the *Fables* being used in the education of his grandson, the Duc de Bourgogne. This must have come about through the intermediary of the great author-archbishop Fénelon, the boy's tutor, who set him to translate La Fontaine into Latin. From the tone of easy familiarity which accompanies the conventional flatteries in the fables concerned (here, XII.1, 2, and 6), it looks as though boy and poet were on terms of friendship. The same is suggested by the prince's behaviour in the last great trial of La Fontaine's life, the episode known as his 'conversion'. The term then meant, not a change from one religion to another, but a resolve to live according to pious rather than worldly values. La Fontaine was ill, and was persuaded by a young abbé to convert in this sense. It involved making a public statement of remorse for writing the notorious *Contes*, which was done in 1693, before a deputation from the Académie. An edition of the work happened to be in press. La Fontaine declared that he would abandon any earnings from it; the young duke, hearing of this, sent him the munificent gift of fifty *louis d'or*, apparently on his own initiative.

Mme de La Sablière's death occurred in the middle of the conversion affair, and her poet was offered accommodation and care by the wealthy son of a friend from the time of Fouquet, the banker d'Hervart, in whose house he was to die in April 1695. When undressed for burial, he was found to be wearing the garment of penitence, a hairshirt. Some eighteen months earlier, but dated 1694, the last volume of fables had been published, under the title *Fables choisies*—somewhat misleading, since about half the volume is taken up by longer narratives, *contes* in fact (though only one is at all salacious). When publicly repudiating those he had already written, he had promised not to publish any more. The very last fable, misanthropic in mood, could be intended as a final gesture towards his good angel: dismissive of a career in law, by which he had not been tempted, but admiring of good works in medical care, like hers, and advocating retreat to pious meditation in the manner of the Jansenist 'solitaries' with whom both he and she were in sympathy.

A Student of Human Behaviour

At a time when La Fontaine was in trouble, the generosity of the prince and of d'Hervart and his wife typifies his situation during most of his career. Often mischievous, viewed with distrust by the established authorities in both Church and State, he could invariably, it seems, elicit affection and practical help from friends. But much of his character is elusive, though intriguing, as biographers frequently observe. One of the paradoxes is that this charming person, so heedless of his own material interests, would choose the fable genre for his best work, a genre professing to give wise advice on how to live.

The upshot is that relating the *Fables* to the character of their creator is extremely difficult. Are there any subjects on which we can say: 'This clearly his own opinion'? The short answer is 'Very seldom', with one obvious exception: when the subject is poetry and poets. Apart from that, greed for money is perhaps the only important topic on which the satire does seem—it is more an impression than anything else—to have a personal edge. It is true that criticism of miserliness was common in satirical writing; in both Molière and Boileau, for instance, it is vigorously ridiculed. Nonetheless, La Fontaine's treatment of it is, for him, exceptionally fierce (see especially VIII.27: 'The Wolf and the Huntsman', IV.20: 'The Miser who Lost his Treasure', and V.13: 'The Hen that Laid the Eggs of Gold'). Since he was in life notorious for dissipating his fortune, the denunciation may well come from the heart.

Money is denounced in the *Fables* largely because its ownership, or the pursuit of it, is destructive of pleasure; there is a hedonistic strain in the work, which no doubt also reflects the poet's temperament. In literary terms, its expression can often be traced back to Lucretius.[5] The cobbler's happiness (VIII.2) turns to constant anxiety on acquiring money from his rich neighbour. So too with the Eastern couple in 'The Wishes' (VII.5). The authorial voice in VIII.27 follows up with advice to those who only want to store up more wealth (or in this case food): 'Enjoy yourself today!' Probably we should deduce,

---

[5] Explored by, among others, David Lee Rubin, *A Pact with Silence: Art and Thought in the* Fables *of Jean de La Fontaine* (Columbus, Ohio, 1992), ch. 2.

not so much that he advocates crude hedonism, but is advising us to be content with what we have rather than seeking more. In the early fable on death (I.15), he aligns himself with the model of all patrons, Maecenas, in asserting that life remains worth living even in illness and disability; the woodcutter in the next fable comes to the same conclusion. A later fable on the same subject (VIII.1) contains a passage in which La Fontaine appears to speak in his own person when saying that the old man should leave life 'as if it were | a banquet where he was a guest, | thanking his host'.

Elsewhere, the identity of author and opinion is doubtful. You can find attacks on marriage, such as 'The Man who Married Badly' (VII.2), as might be expected given La Fontaine's own record (here, pretending to be unmarried, he toys unconvincingly with the notion of an ideal wife), but married life, like greed, has always been a popular target for satirists. La Fontaine himself had already said a great deal to disparage it in the *Contes*, but sexual misdemeanours, their standard topic, are absent from the *Fables*. As for women, the La Fontaine of the *Fables* is not above resorting to traditional jibes, as in the very funny 'Women and Secrets' (VIII.6), but in 'The Drowned Woman' (III.16) the attitude is different. Here he distances himself from the unpleasant male remarks he records, because 'women are our joy'. That women readily forget old loves is a recurrent theme, but it is not necessarily criticized; he discussed 'The Young Widow' (VI.21) with Maucroix, in one of the few notes to him that has survived, and explains that the widow is sincere both in mourning her dead husband and in deciding to remarry. This suggests approval for her realism rather than denunciation.

The note also shows the difficulty of pronouncing on the 'meaning' of any single fable: if even Maucroix needed an explanation, how can anyone now be definite about such matters? However, in the many significant passages concerning the writing of fables and the position of the poet in society, things are plainer. La Fontaine is speaking for himself here. He took from Phaedrus the idea of devoting the first fable of each book, or part of it, to these and related subjects, and in the first collection does so in all except perhaps Book IV. The first poem of Book V, for instance, records agreement between poet and patron on stylistic matters, and so illustrates a proper relation between the two. The same topic is pursued else-where. The early fable (I.14) about the poet Simonides shows him treated badly by an unfair patron, who suffers divine punishment for his meanness. The fable drives the lesson home in its conclusion, in mythological code. Royalty and aristocracy (the dwellers on Olympus) should grant not only material assistance to poets, but also esteem and friendship. A comparable message is conveyed by the very first fable, the importance of which is belied by its apparent slightness. In it the songful cricket's plea for charity is rejected by the miserly ant. On what grounds? —that singing is a waste of the time that should be spent on working. Read: the poet entertains, which the mean-spirited ant does not regard as work, and must depend on patronage, which she wrongly refuses. The message defending the cricket is the more remarkable because La Fontaine's readers would have known the biblical passage (Proverbs 6:6) which his ant virtually personifies: 'Go to the ant, thou sluggard: consider her ways and be wise.'

In other words, there is much suggestive ambiguity in many of these apparently straightforward little tales. Many critics, also, prefer not to decide between conflicting attitudes found in the same fable, on the grounds that author and text should be kept separate and that the fable confines itself to presenting the conflict without resolving it.[6] Despite the doubts concerning La Fontaine's own opinions, this seems to be going too far. Everything in the first fable indicates support for the cricket, which may seem perverse, but consequently makes it hard to sympathize with the ant, whose last words amount to a death sentence. Similarly, when the independent wolf (I.5) faces the tame dog, who (as in Phaedrus) is embarrassed and evasive about wearing a collar, it is difficult not to side with him; in the last line 'he is running still', so has survived the risks of freedom that the dog exchanges for an easy life.

However, we should not conclude that in every fable, or even most, we are given a definite lesson. The 'moral' may well be a topic for discussion rather than an authoritative pronouncement, which the corresponding element in the traditional Aesopic fable, the epimythium,

---

[6] Many examples can be found in Marie-Odile Sweetser, *La Fontaine* (Boston: Twayne, 1987), ch. 2.

often is. In his preface, La Fontaine explains that in following his models he has altered or even dispensed with the moral element when he could not easily fit it in 'gracefully' or to his own satisfaction. In practice, the moral may simply be a more or less serious comment on the story, and in the later fables it often becomes quite lengthy passages of reflection, the story being merely a starting-point. Occasionally we are invited to supply a lesson ourselves. In 'The Cat and the Two Sparrows' (XII.2) La Fontaine plays with the idea, saying both that there should be a moral, and that he cannot see what it might be. It should be remembered also that 'la morale', at the time, was not restricted to what is now understood by morality, but covered also what we might better understand as psychology. To be a *moraliste*, in seventeenth-century France, did not mean being judgemental or sermonizing, but rather being a student of all aspects of human nature and behaviour.[7] The fable's 'instruction' covered lessons about the realities of life, the kind of knowledge, La Fontaine says in his preface, that children cannot yet know by experience.

What he does not mention is that, in the animal fables, which are the majority, the portrayal of life is bleak. They are typically based on the contrast between a stronger and a weaker creature, often predator and prey. The expectation is that the weaker one will be overcome and destroyed unless it can escape, but its chances are limited. Here the archetype is 'The Wolf and the Lamb' (I.10); by rights the lamb's arguments should prevail, but, as we are told at the outset, rightness counts for less than strength. A few fables earlier (I.6), the lion has reminded his allies of the point: 'you must have heard that might is right'. There are many other illustrations (here, I.8; III.5; IV.21; V.3; X.3; XII.5). The variations are more numerous still: in I.2 the fox prevails by cunning, not greater power; in II.4 the bull intends no harm to the frogs but tramples them just the same; in II.9 the fly cannot be hurt by the lion, but meets his fate in a spider's web; and so on. Where destruction can be avoided, it is by using one's wits, which the crow should have done in I.2. The trusting goat in III.5 ought in theory to do the same, but unfortunately lacks the wit to do so, as the fox callously observes.

---

[7] A point well made by Odette de Mourgues, *La Fontaine*: Fables (London: Arnold, 1960), 84.

These are all instances of the 'law of the jungle', the catchphrase frequently used to denote the lawlessness of La Fontaine's animal world. Project it on to human society, and you have a Hobbesian image of 'the war of every man against every man', every human being competing for survival against all the rest, like the beasts. The image is taken up in XII.1 by the wolf: 'you men behave like wolves to other men'. This was something of a commonplace among the stricter moralists, amongst whom the Jansenists are the best-known. A powerful but persecuted movement, Jansenism emphasized the sinfulness of human nature and the necessity of divine grace if we are to be truly good; it was most famously expressed in Pascal's *Pensées*, of 1670. La Rochefoucauld, who had La Fontaine's allegiance, and his tutor at the Oratoire, Desmares, were both influenced by it. He declares his debt to La Rochefoucauld, in both an early and a late fable (I.11; X.14). The fables 'mirror' human nature, he says; men behave like animals, much though they may dislike the idea. Most of us, furthermore—this is from the end of 'Odysseus and his Companions' (XII.1) —would enjoy the brutish life if we could get it.

The implied image of human nature is, then, quite in keeping with Jansenism, but only in summary, and in purely abstract terms. The dark picture is completely altered by La Fontaine's treatment of his material. For one thing, there are many animal fables in which the ruthless law of the jungle fails to operate effectively. In some, the weaker animals escape. Whereas the truthful donkey perishes in VII.1 (which is an attack on the court and courtiers), a stag, facing a similar threat from the lion's court, cleverly lies his way out of trouble (VIII.14); the crow is tricked out of his cheese in I.2, but the cock, facing another fox in II.15, turns the tables. Elsewhere, the struggle for survival becomes comic with the 'humane' wolf overcome by vegetarian remorse (X.5), only to rescind his good resolutions on observing how humans behave. Generally, the humour which accompanies disaster for this or that hapless creature much reduces any pathos, often because the victim has been dim-witted. There is a generalized morality here, and it is the one traditional to the fable. It was a popular genre, more folktale than literature, not destined for the rich and powerful, but for ordinary people, the weak and the unimportant. The constant lesson concerned self-preservation in a rough and unpredictable world. Prudence, caution, and the avoidance of trouble were the watchwords. The Fables express the same attitude in various ways, but the remark at the end of 'The Wolf, the Nanny-Goat, and her Kid' (IV.15), 'precautions can't be overdone', would serve as motto for many other fables.

In the fables involving humans and animals together, a large group, the roles are modified. The overriding theme is exploitation by men, whose behaviour is that of a stronger predator, as in 'The Fisherman and the Little Fish' (V.3). 'The Man and the Snake' (X.1), again, is a version of 'The Wolf and the Lamb', but it turns into a lengthy denunciation of the suffering inflicted on animals, and also trees, by their human masters. Little humour relieves the mood. If we are look-ing for the opinions of the real La Fontaine, we could plausibly argue that they are to be found here. A different picture again emerges from the many fables concerning human society alone. Here there is a much larger degree of realism (perhaps caricature might be a better term), when credulity is portrayed in 'The Soothsayers' (VII.14) or duplicity in 'The Unfaithful Guardian' (IX.1). These show La Fon-taine the satirist. Their subject-matter is individual human failings, but, whatever the animal fables might imply about humans, men are not shown here as bloodthirsty creatures bent on slaughter. War is not often mentioned (as a subject, it appears in a fable, IV.6, about creatures not of great concern, 'The Battle of the Weasels and the Rats'); murder and serious crime not at all. La Fontaine provides a list of his targets in the prologue to IX.1. They are not the worst faults in human nature and are usually, apart from avarice, viewed tolerantly. Compared to satirists such as Swift or Juvenal, or his contemporary Boileau, La Fontaine is gentle, writing not to arouse indignation, but amusement.

In various respects, then, the didactic element in the *Fables* plays a subordinate role. The poet does not wish to be a schoolmaster, a figure derided in 'The Boy and the Schoolmaster' (I.19), where one of them moralizes at the wrong moment.

However, another ancient tendency in fable, to side with the weak against the strong, is maintained. There are exceptions—the lion, though tyrannical, often shows dignity, and can himself be a victim; the oak (I.22) is compassionate as well as arrogant— but the stories usually invite us to side with the humbler members of society and those who suffer oppression. In the fables directly about human society, perhaps the best example is 'The Gardener and his Lord' (IV.4), one of the very few which La Fontaine must have invented. The gardener, who is the victim, could be said to be imprudent in calling for help at all (like other characters, he should have known better), but it is the lord's coarse and callous behaviour that is the target. On an altogether different scale, 'The Danube Peasant' (XI.7) is a prolonged speech against Roman oppression, no doubt with contemporary relevance.[8]

Storytelling

What of La Fontaine's other professed aim, *plaire*, to attract and entertain? About this he never wavered. The Aesopic fable, by definition unrealistic, has intrinsically attractive qualities. It is brief, for one thing, and although for La Fontaine brevity in itself is not the be-all and end-all of the genre, he keeps one of its essentials, the firm closure of the narrative. But he allows himself enough space to develop another feature, the clearly defined, simple characters, often found in contrasting pairs. These qualities act in combination. The definite ending is usually the outcome of conflict between two characters, less often through misfortune due to the leading trait of a single character (the downfall of the oak, in I.22, comes into this category). The advantage of the animal fable is that the basis of character is already given, together with some narrative expectation: the fox will deceive, the wolf will seek prey, the lion will tyrannize, and so on. Some of the most popular and longlasting stories depend on obvious physical features, such as the fox's short muzzle and the stork's long beak in I.18. These enable them to trick each other, the basis of the fable, but La Fontaine's treatment develops it into a little social drama, the fox becoming a local dignitary who behaves with condescension to a humbler neighbour and is duly discomfited. In 'The Hare and the Tortoise' (VI.10), slowness and speed are the basics, the race an utterly unreal narrative device that puts them into action. Some way

---

[8] See Georges Couton, *La Politique de La Fontaine* (Paris: Les Belles Lettres, 1959), 92–5.

must be found to give the absurd outcome at least a semblance of plausibility, but La Fontaine does more: he takes the opportunity to create character-sketches, fecklessness and bravado as against stolid persistence. 'The Fox and the Crow' (I.2) has a particularly successful combination of features: a bird with a big beak, who is of course out of the fox's reach because he can perch on a tree, but ugly and with an ugly voice. He is open to the fox's expert (and delightful) flattery, but unlikely to arouse sympathy when he falls for it.

Something similar, as regards the interplay of character and plot, is found in the human fables. Often the protagonists are defined by one leading trait or by their social role, which determines the direction of the story. The miser, caring only about his treasure, is readymade for stories about losing it (IV.20; IX.16); the fortune-teller's story will concern the credulity of her clients (pointed up in 'The Soothsayers' (VII.14) by the second one's bewilderment at her new role); the doctor, naturally, is going to preside over the demise of his patient (V.12); the lawyer, always rapacious, will benefit at the expense of his client (IX.9), and so on. But in some of this group the formula does not apply, notably in the very last fable, in which doctor and lawyer are well-intentioned, but also, for instance, in an Oriental tale, 'The Two Adventurers and the Talisman' (X.13), which La Fontaine may have chosen precisely because its message, about the rewards of boldness, is unlike any of the rest.

Whatever the appeal of each of his fables taken on its own, La Fontaine took care to ensure that it was not diminished by repetition of the same effect: *diversité* again. In miscellanies, and in this regard the *Fables* are a miscellany, variety is of the essence. This is why the occasional attempts by scholars to establish some principle of unity in the work are bound to fail. The only principle is that in any sequence of fables the tone, the structure of the narrative, the degree of seriousness, and so on, will differ continuously. Apart from a few paired fables, put together usually for reasons of contrast, there are few that resemble at all closely, in subject-matter or in nature, those that precede and follow. A proverb-fable, adapted to be a joke against grandiloquence, will follow sober advice (V.9 and 10), a very complicated riddle follows animal comedy (II.19 and 20). Probably the nearest approach to unity comes in Book I, where La Fontaine was still feeling his way and largely staying with fables selected by Phaedrus, but even here, after a sequence entirely of animal stories, the diversity gradually increases.

In respect of the telling, a fable may be direct quasi-historical summary ('The Battle of the Weasels and the Rats', IV.6), or largely told in dialogue ('The Swallow and the Little Birds', I.8), or by interior monologue ('The Hare and the Frogs', II.14). Usually they are in mixed mode, in other words variety of narration takes over within the fable, rather than from one to the next. 'The Cat and an Old Rat' (III.18) is a comparatively straightforward example, on a subject treated in hundreds of such tales, cat versus rat. It has a narrator figure portraying his main character[9] in hyperbolic language, admiring his trickery; then more or less unadorned narrative of incident; then a mixture of speech and action, ending with the cat's triumph; this seems to be the end, but is followed by a shorter complementary tale with a contrasting outcome but the same combination of character description, incident, and speech.

The style used in this example is perhaps the only feature which recurs throughout a sequence of fables otherwise different. It has great flexibility; the differing lengths of line that La Fontaine usually employs, in irregular combination, give an effect of greater naturalness than any standard metrical pattern. He moves constantly, from line to line and sometimes within the line, from the more to the less formal, from narratorial comment to action, from description to dialogue. 'The Cat, the Weasel, and the Little Rabbit' (VII.15) shows La Fontaine's skill in this style at its fullest development. Here simple variety of effect often becomes something more, a series of tiny surprises contrived by expert handling of the reader's expectations. 'Palace' and 'rabbit', put together, do not fit: the incongruous overstatement is instantly followed by the invasion that initiates the story, the weasel also being treated hyperbolically ('household gods'). 'The easy way' needs explanation, which we get: the rabbit was not at home; but the bare fact is amplified, unexpectedly, by two lines of pure lyricism. Then the tone changes to gently ironic description as

---

[9] Who in literary terms is the ancestor of Puss-in-Boots: Perrault, no doubt in homage to La Fontaine, ascribes the same tricks to his cat hero in *Le Chat botté*.

the rabbit browses, before he has the shock of finding the weasel in possession. And so on, through a legal debate raising basic questions about property, suited to the situation in human terms, but which could not be predicted from the story's opening, until the description of the sinister cat prepares the brutal ending. A final twist comes in the moral comment, which is not about the characters, but widens the perspective to 'mighty states'; this comment in retrospect picks up some implications about invasion and conquest made in the legal argument.

In such a fable as this, and many others, the intrinsic qualities of the traditional fable (in this case from the *Pañcatantra*) are still easily discernible, but its potentialities have been exploited so far as to make it virtually a different genre, unique to La Fontaine. He was said from the beginning to be inimitable, and so it has proved; later attempts have fallen far short of their would-be model.[10] His originality was of a kind that may be hard to comprehend today. It did not mean creating an original story, but making a given story his own through comment, dialogue, and variation in tone: those many 'little touches' that he tells us, modestly but evasively, he adds to what he found in Aesop and elsewhere. These devices are too many to enumerate and so ingeniously combined that they are often hard to separate in commentary: better simply to recommend that they are read, in the hope that La Fontaine's mastery can still, even in translation, achieve some of the effect that he claims: 'stories cast a magic spell' (II.1). But, as he implies, story on its own does not suffice; skill in the telling is required. The 'wondrous art' of Homer and Aesop to which he pays tribute (IX.1) is also there for us to appreciate in the *Fables*.

---

[10] Charles Perrault, the author of the famous fairy tales, has the best claim to be a disciple, but in the fable form he never rose to the same level. The fable genre created by La Fontaine inspired French poets throughout the eighteenth century, from La Mothe Houdart at the beginning to Florian at the end, but their narratives are more didactic than those of their master.

NOTE ON THE TRANSLATION

❦

The Explanatory Notes at the back of the book give information on allusions and expressions that may be obscure; each is signalled by an asterisk in the text. They also include, for every fable, its French title and its source, or a note on the historical background when a textual source does not exist. Almost all the sources have been established by scholars over many years; their value is that to compare La Fontaine's version with his source is almost always illuminating. For both text and notes, and for the numbering of the fables, the French editions of the *Fables* that I have mainly used are those by Georges Couton (Paris: Garnier, 1962), Marc Fumaroli (Paris: Livre de poche, 1985), and Jean-Pierre Collinet (Paris: Gallimard, 1991).

I have included roughly half of the total number of fables: 237 is the usual count in the twelve Books published by La Fontaine. The total will differ slightly depending on whether some of the paired fables are counted as one or two, and if the fables in Book XII that are in effect *contes* are excluded. A few survive that he did not publish, none of which is included here. The aim has been to include as wide a range as possible of the various kinds of fable that can be distinguished. Apart from the different categories based on character, animals, humans, or gods, or a combination, there are for instance puzzle fables (II.20, 'Aesop's Explanation of a Will'), epigram fables, to use Fumaroli's term, such as the 'sour grapes' fable (III.11) or 'Death and the Unhappy Man' (I.15), recording a famous remark by Maecenas, and fables that are more like a *conte*, but shorter than those to which La Fontaine gave the name, such as 'The Middle-Aged Man and his Two Loves' (I.17) or 'The Young Widow' (VI.21).

On the scale of simple entertainment to serious reflection (for example, 'The Acorn and the Pumpkin', IX.4, and 'The Astrologer in the Well', II.13), I have tried to ensure a proper balance, in the belief that to keep to the lighter end of the scale would in the end be less interesting. I have included almost all the first and last fables in each of the twelve books, which seem to have been prominently placed because La Fontaine regarded them as important in various ways, and almost all of the fables concerning England. All the fables here are complete, with the proviso that the last fable in Book IX, 'The Two Rats, the Fox, and the Egg', though complete in itself, is an extract (see the accompanying note); in other words, I have not omitted dedications, etc., when they are an integral part of the piece, as with IV.1, 'The Lion in Love'.

There are virtually no textual problems, except that modern French editions may differ over punctuation, which has changed somewhat since the seventeenth century. It is not known whether the original editions have La Fontaine's punctuation or that habitual to the printer. In doubtful cases I have used my discretion. There have been many previous translations into English, on both sides of the Atlantic, probably the best known being by Sir Edward Marsh, Marianne Moore, Norman Shapiro, James Michie, and Christopher Wood, all of which, and others, I have consulted with profit, but have not knowingly imitated except where annotation is concerned, and here I have been much helped by Shapiro's notes and by those in the Wood translation by Maya Slater.

From the first it has been usual where possible to illustrate the *Fables*; the plates in the early editions, at a time when people did not enjoy the plethora of images that we take for granted now, counted for a lot in making the volumes attractive. The most famous are the original plates by François Chauveau, by Jean-Baptiste Oudry in the eighteenth century, by Gustave Doré in the nineteenth, and Marc Chagall in the twentieth (see in the Select Bibliography the items by Chauveau and Bassy and the lafontaine.net website). The selection included here, from the centenary edition of 1868, shows Doré at his best, still in monochrome like his predecessors, but more detailed than Chauveau and more vigorous than Oudry.

La Fontaine's verse is in form strict by modern standards, though not by those of his own time. I have tried to follow his practice. He always observes the rule of alternation of rhyme; it had to alternate between feminine, those ending with the French mute -e (which would then have been pronounced in verse read aloud), and masculine, those ending in any other way. For this there is not much that is comparable in English, except possibly the difference between rhymes on the stressed final syllable and those on the two last when the stress falls on the penultimate: *meant* and *intent* as against *follow* and *swallow*. Although I have used the latter sort of rhyme when conveni- ent or appropriate, the regular alternation of the two sorts would, I think, seem tiresome—quite apart from its intrinsic difficulty. Like La Fontaine I occasionally use a triple rhyme. That, for French poetry at the time, was informal, like his free use of different lengths of line within the same poem. His normal usage is to mix up the 12-syllable alexandrine, standard in French for serious verse, with lines of 10 or (more commonly) 8 syllables, which give a lighter impression. The obviously corresponding choice in English, which counts by stress rather than syllable, is to combine the iambic pentameter with the octosyllabic line. La Fontaine sometimes chooses a stricter scheme, for instance staying with the same metre throughout, and in such cases I have if possible done the same. In some passages which seem to call for it I have resorted to the un-English alexandrine, and at the other extreme have imitated his occasional playful use of a very short line.

Such are the technical details, or some of them; the essence of the matter is that, although for a fluent versifier the easy option is to add a line or two in order to convey meaning, or in other words to resort to padding, La Fontaine seldom does so. It is not exactly that he aims only at brevity; the quality the *Fables* possess is rather concision, the ability to pack much matter into few words. 'Not a word is wasted': the banal praise is here deserved. For the translator, the need to pad out, for the sake of metre and rhyme, is almost constant, yet doing so dilutes the sense, and to my mind often reduces the suggestive power of the poetry. For this reason I have tried wherever I could to equate our ten-syllable line with the French alexandrine, or at least, since all too often I have not managed it, to put La Fontaine's half-line units— the alexandrine had to have a break after the sixth syllable—into an octosyllable. He does of course often carry the sense over from one line to the next, although such *enjambement* was frowned on; here the problems of translation are somewhat easier.

La Fontaine's verse, partly through flexibility in rhyme and metre, succeeds in giving an impression of naturalness and ease, despite the innate artificiality of the form. That must be another aim for the translator, however unattainable it seems. The same applies with one of the most fascinating characteristics of his fables, their variety of tone and register, not always but often changing rapidly, even within a line. In general, I have aimed at a style which is on the formal side, since although many characters in the *Fables* speak in colloquial idiom, it is clearly distinguished from the prevailing style of the narrator. La Fontaine sometimes affects slight archaism, which should not, I think, encourage the translator to employ such expressions as *fain would I*, *ne'er*, and so on, which are convenient but too quaint, and I have avoided as far as possible the 'poetic' inversion of object and verb, as in (one I could not avoid) 'The King of Beasts an order gave' (VI.14). I have resorted to inversions such as 'to leave their holes they did not dare' (II.2) when necessary.

Another feature typical of La Fontaine, the quality he calls 'lightness and grace' (*grâces légères*, VIII, 4, *léger* suggesting both delicacy and a lack of seriousness), which is a delight for the reader, is the translator's despair. Although lightness of mood can be caught, the grace in movement of La Fontaine's poetry is seldom imitable. Grace, he wrote when describing Venus in his *Adonis*, is 'plus belle encor [*sic*] que la beauté', more beautiful even than beauty, because, I think, it suggests motion rather than stillness. He takes full advantage of the fluidity and evenness of the French language, against which English, with its more definite accentuation, complex vowel sounds, and massed consonants, tends to sound heavy. The more colloquial and humorous passages do not necessarily suffer too much, but when La Fontaine is in lyrical mood things become more difficult.

The translator of poems, perhaps more acutely than with prose, is caught between the twin demands of faithfulness in meaning and effectiveness in expression. However, to my mind the decision which to favour is usually more straightforward. Whenever I have felt that there was a genuine conflict, which often happens when rhyme is a pressing problem, I have almost invariably preferred to sacrifice some nuance of meaning rather than to end up with something clumsy or awkward. Anyone who takes the trouble to look will be able to find plenty of examples of both, as well as of inexact transmission of meaning, but will, I hope, believe me when I say that I am all too aware of them and have tried without success to find something better.

My efforts to do so have been much aided by various friends and acquaintances. Librarians first of all: I should like to thank those at the Taylorian Library in Oxford for frequent assistance. To a group of kind friends in Charlbury I am indebted for putting up with having sample translations read to them, a most valuable service, and even, moreover, finding words of encouragement. I am also grateful for encouragement and advice to Gaston Hall, Michael Schmidt, Michael Hawcroft, and especially Peter France; and for help with matters Aesopic to Laura Gibbs. To Judith Luna as editor I (like so many others) am deeply obliged, to start with for believing that the project was worth pursuing, later for invaluable discussions of detail, and in particular, as before with Perrault, for managing the problems posed by Doré's splendid illustrations. Translating La Fontaine is addictive, as Norman Shapiro, who put all the *Fables* into English, explained eloquently in his Preface; it is to my wife Ann's acceptance that I would have to work through the addiction that I owe the most. Without her unobtrusive and resolute support, the undertaking would not have come to fruition.

SELECT BIBLIOGRAPHY

There are numerous books on La Fontaine in French. Here I give a limited selection of works mostly in English. For details of the French editions of the *Fables* that I have used, by Couton, Collinet, and Fumaroli, all of which contain valuable introductions as well as full annotation, see the Note on the Translation.

Works on La Fontaine and the Fables

Bassy, Alain-Marie, *Les* Fables *de La Fontaine: Quatre siècles d'illustration* (Paris, c.1996).

Biard, Jean-Dominique, *The Style of La Fontaine's Fables* (Oxford, 1966).

Birberick, Anne L., *Refiguring La Fontaine, Tercentenary Essays* (Charlottesville, Virginia, 1996).

Calder, Andrew, *The Fables of La Fontaine, Wisdom Brought Down to Earth* (Geneva, 2001).

Chauveau, François, ed. J.-D. Biard, *Vignettes des Fables de La Fontaine (1668)* (Exeter, 1977).

Dandrey, Patrick, *La Fontaine ou les Métamorphoses d'Orphée* (Paris, 1995).

Danner, Richard, *Patterns of Irony in the Fables of La Fontaine* (Athens, Ohio, 1985).

de Mourgues, Odette, *La Fontaine:* Fables (London, Arnold, 1960).

Duchêne, Roger, *Jean de La Fontaine* (Paris, 1990). Biography.

Fumaroli, Marc, translated by Jane Marie Todd, *The Poet and the King, Jean de La Fontaine and his Century* (Notre Dame, Indiana, 2002).

Guiton, Margaret, *La Fontaine, Poet and Counterpoet* (New Brunswick, NJ, 1961).

Gutwirth, Marcel, *Un Merveilleux sans éclat: La Fontaine ou la Poésie exilée* (Geneva, 1987).

Rubin, David Lee, *A Pact with Silence: Art and Thought in the Fables of Jean de La Fontaine* (Columbus, Ohio, 1991).

Slater, Maya, *The Craft of La Fontaine* (London and Madison, 2000–1).

Spitzer, Leo, 'The Art of Transition in La Fontaine', in *Essays on 17th-Century French Literature*, trans. David Bellos (Cambridge, 1983), 169–207.

Sweetser, Marie-Odile, *La Fontaine* (Boston, 1987).

Wadsworth, Philip, *Young La Fontaine: A Study of his Artistic Growth in his Early Poetry and First Fables* (Evanston, Illinois: Northwestern University Press, 1952).

Further General Reading

Babrius and Phaedrus, trans. and ed. Ben Edwin Perry (Cambridge, Mass., and London, 1965).

Blackham, H. J., *The Fable as Literature* (London, 1985).

The Complete Fables of Jean de La Fontaine, trans. and ed. Norman Shapiro (Urbana and Chicago, 2007).

Jean de La Fontaine, The Complete Tales in Verse, trans. and ed. Guido Waldman (Manchester, 2000).

Lewis, Jayne Elizabeth, *The English Fable: Aesop and Literary Culture, 1651–1740* (Cambridge, 1996).

Further Reading in Oxford World's Classics

Aesop's Fables, trans. and ed. Laura Gibbs.

La Rochefoucauld, François de, *Collected Maxims and Other Reflections*, trans. E. H. and A. M. Blackmore, introduction by Francine Giguère.

The Pañcatantra, The Book of India's Folk Wisdom, trans. and ed. Patrick Olivelle.

Pascal, Blaise, *Pensées and Other Writings*, trans. Honor Levi, ed. Anthony Levi.

Perrault, Charles, *The Complete Fairy Tales*, trans. and ed. Christopher Betts.

Websites

http://mythfolklore.net/aesopica (Laura Gibbs's site containing virtually all known versions of Aesopic fables, together with translations in many instances).

http://www.lafontaine.net/nouveau-site (in French; concerns all aspects of La Fontaine's work, with texts, and has collections of illustrations to the *Fables*).

A CHRONOLOGY OF JEAN DE LA FONTAINE

꿏꿏

1621 (8 July) Baptism at Château-Thierry of Jean de La Fontaine, first son of a prosperous bourgeois father. He has a half-sister, his mother's daughter by her first marriage, who leaves home to marry in 1627, and a brother, Claude, born 1623.

from c.1632 Attends the well-reputed college of Château-Thierry, where possibly he meets François de Maucroix (1619–1708), who was to be a canon of Rheims cathedral and LF's closest friend; then (from c.1635) a college in Paris.

1641 Studies with the Oratorians, a forward-looking religious order, while apparently considering a career in the Church; his brother joins him in October 1641, and stays to become a priest; LF leaves a year later and returns home.

1644 Probable date of the death of his mother.

1645–7 Studies law at Paris and becomes a member of the 'Table ronde', a group of young writers, led by the older Paul Pellisson and including Maucroix and Furetière, another friend who was to become a writer.

1647 (November) Contract of marriage between LF and Marie Héricart (1633–1709), a cousin of the dramatist Jean Racine (1639–99); the marriage is believed to be of LF's father's making.

1652 LF becomes, like his father, 'maître particulier des eaux et forêts' for Château-Thierry and Châtillon-sur-Marne, a government post which provides a stable but limited income.

1653 (30 October) Baptism at Château-Thierry of Charles (d. 1723), LF's only child; Maucroix stands godfather.

1654 (August) LF's first publication, at Paris, unsigned: *L'Eunuque* ('The Eunuch'), a verse comedy imitated from Terence, which goes unremarked.

1657/8 By now LF and Marie Héricart are believed to be living more or less separately. Gains entry, probably through his wife's uncle Jacques Jannart, to the circle of Nicolas Fouquet, Louis XIV's finance minister, a rich patron of the arts, who employs both Jannart and Pellisson.

1658 (April) Death of LF's father, bringing problems in the administration of the estate, apparently dealt with by Jannart.

1659 Fouquet commissions from LF, now writing regularly for him, a poem in honour of his magnificent residence, Vaux-le-Vicomte: *Le Songe de Vaux* ('The Dream of Vaux').

1660–1 LF becomes a friend of Racine. At this time he is living partly in Paris, often at Jannart's house, and partly in Château-Thierry.

1661 (August–September) Fouquet gives a sumptuous reception at Vaux for the king, at which LF is present; soon after, Fouquet is arrested, imprisoned on charges of financial peculation, and detained for the rest of his life: a serious blow for LF, who continues to write for a while in his support.

1663 (August) Jannart, as a close associate of Fouquet's, is temporarily exiled to Limoges, accompanied by LF, whether compulsorily or not is unknown.

1664 Becomes a member of the household of the dowager duchess of Orléans, until 1672, and now has the privileged status of *gentilhomme*, while continuing to lodge with Jannart in Paris. In salon society he mixes with other writers such as Mme de Sévigné, celebrated for her letters and a friend of Fouquet's, and La Rochefoucauld, whose *Maximes* LF admires.

1665 (January) Publication of the first volume of *Contes*, tales in verse, more or less scurrilous, many from Boccaccio. One of these, *Joconde*, from Ariosto, is much praised by Boileau (1636–1711) in his first critical work. The volume is popular and is followed by a second in 1666 and by three further tales in 1667.

1668 (March) Publication of the first collection of *Fables*, 124 fables in six books; an immediate success.

1669 (January) Publication of *Les Amours de Psyché et de Cupidon* ('Psyche and Cupid in Love'), a romantic mythological novel mainly in prose, which in 1671 becomes the basis of *Psyché*, a popular musical drama, written jointly by Corneille, Molière, Quinault, and Lulli.

1670 Boileau's first *Epître* published; it contains a fable on a subject also used by LF, 'The Oyster and its Claimants' (IX.9).

1671 Publication of a third volume of *Contes*, containing 14 more, and separately eight further fables, later included in the 1678 collection.

1672 Death of the dowager duchess of Orléans; LF no longer has any kind of employment.

c.1673 He is taken in by Mme de La Sablière, by whom he is supported until her death in 1693. She also provides lodging for François Bernier, a writer and traveller from whom LF learns about Oriental fables. Publishes his poem *De la captivité de Saint Malc* ('The Captivity of Saint Malchus', on the saint's resistance to temptation).

1674 He quarrels with the leading operatic composer Lulli, who rejects a libretto by LF, although it has the support of Mme de Montespan, the king's mistress. LF responds by a satirical attack on Lulli, *Le Florentin*. LF's *Nouveaux Contes* are published without official authorization; bawdy tales about the clergy, they are banned by the chief of police in 1675 on grounds of immorality. Boileau publishes his *Art poétique*, in which fables are omitted from his review of poetical genres.

1676 LF sells his family house in Château-Thierry.

1678–9 Publishes the second main collection of *Fables* (Books VII to XI in modern editions) together with the previous ones.

c.1680 Mme de La Sablière, whose lover of many years, La Fare, has left her, devotes herself to charitable work in a hospital, while continuing to provide lodging for LF.

1682 (January) LF publishes his *Poème du Quinquina* ('Poem on Quinine'), together with two new *contes* and other poems.

1683 (May) His play *Le Rendez-vous* is put on at the Comédie Française, but withdrawn after only four performances. (November) As a candidate for a place at the Académie Française, he receives a majority of the votes cast, but Louis XIV declines to ratify his election until, in April 1684, Boileau is elected.

1685 (January) The Académie expels Furetière for presuming to publish his own dictionary in competition with the Académie's; LF is among a deputation sent, unsuccessfully, to ask his old friend to reconsider. The expulsion brings a bitter pamphlet war between him and his opponents, including LF. LF publishes the poems of Maucroix together with some of his own.

1687 Encouraged by friends, he thinks of going to live among the French expatriate community in London, several of whom he knows well, but decides to stay in Paris.

1688–9 Through his familiarity with Mme Ulrich, a close associate of the Vendôme brothers, disreputable relatives of the royal family, he is drawn into their circle at the Temple in Paris.

1690 (December) Publishes the fable *Les Compagnons d'Ulysse* (XII.1, 'Odysseus and his Companions'), dedicated to the Duc de Bourgogne, the grandson of Louis XIV.

1691 (November) His 'lyrical tragedy' *Astrée* is put on at the Opéra but is given only six performances.

1692 (December) While ill he is visited by a young abbé, Poujet, who persuades him to make a general confession involving the repudiation of the *Contes*.

1693 (January) Death of Mme de La Sablière. LF is taken in by a wealthy friend, d'Hervart, and his wife, who will look after him until his death. (February) In front of a deputation from the Académie he declares his remorse for publishing the *Contes*, resolving not to take any profit from their publication in future. The Duc de Bourgogne sends him a large sum as compensation. (September) Publication, dated 1694, of a volume of LF's *Fables choisies*, Book XII in modern editions, containing 10 new fables besides those published since 1678, together with other stories in verse.

1695 (13 April) Death of LF, who had been taken ill in the street in February.

1696 After unenthusiastic tributes have been paid to LF at the Académie, Charles Perrault, the author of the fairy tales, includes him in his biographical compendium *Les Hommes illustres de ce siècle* ('The Illustrious Men of This Century'), warmly praising the *Fables*.

SELECTED FABLES

THE EARLY FABLES

(BOOKS I TO VI, 1668)

THE CRICKET AND THE ANT

A cricket* who had sung her song
    all summer long,
for lack of food was much deprived
    when winter winds arrived.
No fly or grub, however small:
nothing for her to eat at all.
She goes to neighbour ant and pleads:
she's nearly starving; if she may,
she'd like to borrow what she needs:
a little corn, to see her through
until the spring. Says she: 'I'll pay,
on insect's honour, debt and interest too,
    before next August harvest day.'
    The ant is not a lending beast;
    among her failings, that's the least.
    She asks the borrower: 'And what
were you engaged in when the months were hot?'
    'So please you, ma'am, by night and day
    I sang, to all who passed my way.'
'You sang? Well, well,' the ant her neighbour said;
'I'm glad to hear it. Now then, dance instead.'

BOOK I.I

THE FOX AND THE CROW

A crow sat in a tree, high overhead,
and in his beak a cheese was firmly held.
A fox, attracted there because it smelled,
spoke more or less like this. 'Good day!' he said;
'Sir Crow, you are so handsome! For my part
   I've never seen a bird so smart!
   And if your singing is as good,
   then you must be the Phoenix bird,*
   the brightest star in all this wood.'
Unable to contain himself for pride,
the crow, to let his charming voice be heard,
   opened his beak; it opened wide;
   his treasure fell, just at the fox's side.
He seized the cheese, and said: 'My dear old crow:
   a flatterer, you ought to know,
   lives only at his victim's cost.
This lesson's worth, I think, the cheese you've lost.'
The crow, ashamed and cross, could only say
   he'd not be caught again that way.

BOOK I.2

THE FROG WHO WANTED TO BE AS BIG AS AN OX

A frog was looking at an ox, and thought:
   'He has a very splendid figure.'
This frog was small: a chicken's egg was bigger.
   But even so he enviously sought
   to stretch, and to expand and swell,
   intending as his size increased
eventually to match the larger beast.

He asked his neighbour frog: 'Now can you tell
  how far, my friend, I've got to go?
Look carefully. Is that sufficient?'—'No.'
'Is this, then?'—'No, it's not.'—'Well, am I there
  by now?'—'You're nowhere near.'
The puny creature, having tried and tried,
  tried one last time, blew up, and died.

The world shows no more sense in other things:
mere princelings must have embassies,
and citizens want castles; marquesses
want page-boys in their train, like kings.

    BOOK I.3

THE TWO MULES

Two mules were travelling along a road.
One carried oats; cash was the other's load:
the tax on salt;* and this one, feeling proud
to bear a noble burden on his back,
would not for worlds have had a lighter pack.
  His step was high, his bell rang loud.
Then enemies approach: a robber band;
  they want the money, their assault
is on the tax-man's mule. He makes a stand;
they seize his bridle, force him to a halt.
Resisting, he is stabbed by knife and sword.
He groans and sighs: 'Is this then the reward',
he said, 'my masters promised I would get?
My comrade's safe; to him there was no threat;
  but I was caught; I'll soon be dead.'
'Sometimes, my friend,' the other said,
  'it is not good to serve the great;

if you had been a miller's mule instead,
like me, you'd not be in this dreadful state.'

BOOK I.4

THE WOLF AND THE DOG

A wolf was skin and bone; the dogs on guard
performed their duties well, and times were hard.
He chanced to meet a dog one day
who'd carelessly allowed himself to stray.
　　This dog was large, well-covered, trim,
and handsome; if Sir Wolf had had his way
he'd happily have torn him limb from limb;
　　but first there'd have to be a fight,
and since the mastiff, from the look of him,
　　was likely to defend himself with vigour,
　　the wolf decides it's best to be polite,
approaches meekly, starts a conversation,
and compliments the dog; so fine a figure,
　　he says, deserves his admiration.
'Fair Sir, the choice is yours,' the dog responds;
'you too could be well-fed like me. You should
　　abandon living in the wood;
your fellows there are paupers, vagabonds,
　　poor devils in a wretched state;
to starve to death will surely be their fate.
There nobody will serve you dinners free;
you get your food by violence and strife;
there's no security. Come back with me;
you'll have a much more comfortable life.'
'What must I do, then?' asked the wolf. 'Not much,'
　　answered the dog; 'just chase away
beggars and tramps who have a stick or crutch.

Upon the staff you fawn; the master you obey.
They give you in return a lot to eat:
   all sorts of scraps, left-over meat,
with pigeon-bones and chicken-bones to chew.
They often stroke you and caress you too.'
The wolf reflects upon this life of ease,
and weeps to think it could be his to share.
They walk along together; then he sees,
around the other's neck, a strip rubbed bare.
'What's that?' he asks him. 'Nothing.' 'What d'you mean,
it's nothing?' 'Nothing much,' the dog replied.
'There's something, all the same.' 'Perhaps you've seen
the mark my collar makes when I am tied.'
'You're tied?' the wolf exclaimed. 'You cannot go
wherever you might want?' 'Not always, no.
   It's not a thing I mind about.'
   'But I would mind; and so much so,'
   the wolf said, 'that I'll do without
   the meals you're given. Eat your fill;
   to make me want them at that price
   no kind of treasure would suffice.'
With that, the wolf ran off; he's running still.

   BOOK I.5

⇢⇢·❮══════❯·⇠⇠

THE HEIFER, THE GOAT, AND THE SHEEP, IN ALLIANCE WITH THE LION

   A goat, a sheep, a heifer, so we're told,
   joined forces with a lion, fierce and bold,
      the lord of all the land around;
      by firm agreement each was bound:
      their gains and losses would be shared.
   The goat lays traps; a stag is soon ensnared;

she sends to tell the other three to come.
The lion counts his claws to do the sum,
declares: 'That's four of us to share the prize,'
divides it into parts of equal size,
    and takes the first as being lord.
'The reason is,' he says, 'it's my reward
because I am a lion: that's my name;
it cannot be denied. By right, I claim
the second piece as mine; you must have heard
that might is right. And since, in this affair,
I am the bravest, I will take the third.
    Regarding the remaining share,'
the lion said, 'if any one of you
should dare to touch it, she'll be slaughtered too.'

BOOK I.6

THE TWO POUCHES

Said Jupiter one day: 'Now gather round,
    all you who live and breathe; appear
before my mighty presence. If you have found
unpleasing aspects of your size or shape,
    please say so now. Have no fear.
I'll put the matter right. Step forward, ape:
    why you are first is all too clear.
    Compare the beauty of your features
    with those of all the other creatures.
        Are you content with yours?'
        'What, me?' the ape replied;
    'why shouldn't I be satisfied?
I've legs like them for going on all fours;
my portrait doesn't give me cause for shame.
    With brother bear, it's not the same:

he's just a sketch, unfinished; in his place
I wouldn't want a picture of my face.'
The bear came forward next, and all believed
he'd give them reasons why he felt aggrieved.
Not so, however; when he spoke
he said he found the elephant a joke:
    the ears too wide, the tail too short,
a shapeless lump; no charm of any sort.
The elephant, although reputed wise,
    said much the same when he was heard:
    Dame Whale was of too large a size.
Dame Ant, about herself, employed the word
'enormous': mites, she said, were much too small.
So Jove dismissed them. Full of self-content,
but scornful of the rest, back home they went.
For foolish pride, our race excelled them all.
We humans, of whatever rank or kind,
when looking at ourselves, like moles, are blind,
but are lynx-eyed when others meet our gaze;
    no faults of theirs will we condone,
    but every time excuse our own.
We see ourselves and them in different ways.

Almighty God employs a single mould
to make men now the same as men of old.
We're like the beggar with his double sack:
one pouch before, a second at his back.
The first we keep for failings that we find
in fellow-men; our own we put behind.

BOOK I.7

THE SWALLOW AND THE LITTLE BIRDS

A swallow travelled far, and as she flew
all that she saw her memory retained.
By seeing much, much knowledge will be gained.
When storms were coming, great or small, she knew,
 and even when the skies were clear
could warn the sailors if a gale was due.
It chanced that at the season of the year
for sowing hemp, she watched a farmer sow
the many furrows where this crop would grow.
She told the little birds: 'What I see here
is bad; for you the dangers are severe.
I feel much pity for you. As for me,
I'll fly to distant parts, or if I stay*
I'll live in some dark corner. Can you see
that hand which hovers in the air?
 Shortly will come the evil day
when what the farmer spreads around
 will ruin you: you must beware;
 for from that sowing, plants will spring.
Those plants make snares,* to trap you on the ground,
 and nets to trap you on the wing.
Contrivances like these the humans use
to capture you whenever they may choose.
Imprisonment or death will be your fate;
their cages and their cooking-pots await.
And that is why,' the swallow said, 'you need
to follow my advice, and eat that seed.'
The little birds all mocked: they didn't care;
in other fields was plenty and to spare.
And when the hemp grew fine new shoots:
'Pull up those cursed seedlings by their roots,'
she told them; 'otherwise, your fate is sealed.'
'Your prophecies of doom are idle chat,'
they answered her. 'Why should we work like that?

A fine idea you've had, to clear this field!
You'd need a hundred birds, not us alone.'
    Quite soon the hemp was fully grown.
    'The outlook worsens,' said the swallow;
    'these weeds grow quickly when they're sown.
    My counsels you refuse to follow,
    but still I'll add just one thing more:
    for when the fields are sown again
    and leave some leisure to the men,
    their occupation will be war.
With traps and nets they will attack your race.
    You would be well advised to try
    to stay near home, and not to fly
    now here now there, from place to place.
If possible you ought to relocate,
like duck and stork and woodcock, who migrate.
But you are not as powerful as they:
you could not cross the seas and desert sands
    to reach new worlds in far-off lands.
    To be quite safe, the only way
is shelter in a crevice in some wall.'
But now the little birds, becoming bored,
began to chirp and squawk: between them all
    they made as loud a din and babble
as when Cassandra's warnings were ignored:*
her voice was silenced by the Trojan rabble.
    In neither case were many saved:
most of the birds and Trojans were enslaved.

Instinctively behaving as we like
we won't believe in troubles till they strike.

    BOOK I.8

THE TOWN RAT AND THE COUNTRY RAT

THE TOWN RAT AND THE COUNTRY RAT

The town rat asked the country rat,
    politely, if he'd share
some pheasant scraps, both lean and fat;
    at home, he'd some to spare.

Across a carpet from Baghdad
    was spread the splendid treat;
and what a lovely time they had
    with all that food to eat!

Nothing's amiss; it's all just right,
    surroundings and cuisine;
but when the party's at its height
    humans disturb the scene.

Voices outside come to their ears.
    Quicker than you can tell
the town rat turns; he disappears;
    the country rat as well.

But then the humans go away,
    and back come host and guest.
The city dweller says: 'We'll stay,
    and finish off the rest.'

'Enough,' the country rat replied.
    'Next time, pay me a visit;
I cannot boast that I'll provide
    anything so exquisite;

but in my home I eat at leisure:
    no interruptions there.
Goodbye; no feast can be a pleasure
    when it is spoiled by fear.'

BOOK I.9

THE WOLF AND THE LAMB

The reasons given by the strong are best,
   as this example will attest.

A lamb stood in a river, pure and clear,
   quenching his thirst; a wolf came past;
   his hunger brought him prowling there,
   looking for food to break his fast.
    'How dare you brazenly pollute
my drinking place?' exclaimed this raging brute;
   'such insolence must be chastised.'
'Do not be angry, Sire,' replied the lamb;
'Your Majesty, no doubt, has realized
    that standing where I am
I'm more than twenty paces down the stream
   from where you are; it does not seem
   that I disturb, in any way,
   the water you might drink.' 'I say
   you do disturb it, even so,'
the cruel beast responded; 'and I know
   you spoke much ill of me last year.'
'How could I, when I wasn't born? My mother
has not yet weaned me from her milk, I swear.'
'Then if it wasn't you, it was your brother.'
'I haven't got one.'—'Then it must have been
some other of your family that I mean.
   You persecute me—not just you,
   but all your dogs and shepherds too.
For that's what I've been told; it proves my case;
   I'll have revenge.' He took his prey,
and ate him deep in woodland far away;
no trial of any other kind took place.

BOOK I.10

THE MAN AND HIS IMAGE

*For M. le duc de La Rochefoucauld**

A man who loved himself was free
of any rivals. Such a handsome man,
    he thought, there could not be,
    not ever since the world began.
His looking-glass would tell him otherwise,
but he was sure that it was telling lies;
he lived content in this deluded state.
To cure this malady, officious Fate
put everywhere he went, before his eyes,
those mute advisers to the fairer sex,
mirrors: mirrors in homes, mirrors in shops,
    mirrors for ladies' men and fops,
mirrors at women's waists; and all to vex
our new Narcissus.* What was he to do?
    Unable to endure the thought
    that his reflection might be caught
    in glass or mirror, he withdrew;
    he travelled far away to hide
    and live alone. But even here
he finds a stream, its waters sparkling clear,
and in it sees himself. Much mortified,
he makes himself believe, with indignation,
the spectacle is mere imagination.
He tries to turn away, but fails: the sight
of running water brings him such delight
he cannot leave the beauty of the stream.

My meaning will be clear: I speak to all.
In each of us, excessive self-esteem
is the deluded state in which we fall,
a malady that we enjoy; our soul
is here the man who loves himself alone,
and others' faults the mirrors, since their role

is to portray those defects of our own
   at which we struggle not to look.
As for the sparkling stream, it is a book
   that everyone who reads will know,
   the *Maxims* of La Rochefoucauld.

BOOK I.11

THE DRAGON WITH MANY HEADS AND THE DRAGON WITH MANY TAILS

According to historical report,
the Turkish envoy to the Imperial Court
once spoke of warfare, saying he preferred
the forces that the Sultan had to those
   of which the Empire could dispose.
   A German who was there demurred:
'Our Holy Roman Emperor is lord
of mighty princes; they can each afford
to set on foot an army all complete.'
'I know,' said the vizier, a man of sense,
'I know from common talk how much expense
   your princes can or cannot meet;
   and your remarks recall to me
a spectacle I witnessed which must be
the strangest happening ever seen, though true.
I saw a hydra, many-headed, reaching through
a sturdy hedge towards me, and although
   I was in safety, even so
   I felt my blood run cold. I'd guess
   that many have been scared by less.
But I escaped unhurt; there was no need
to feel such fear; the beast could not proceed;
its heads were through the gaps, the body caught.
   As I reflected, deep in thought,

approaching me I saw another beast,
and just as strange: this dragon had one head,
one body, but with twenty tails at least.
    And while I watched in fear and dread,
its head went through, the body next, and last
    the many tails. Each part in line
    opened the way; the others passed
unhindered, each in turn. Now I would claim
that as between your emperor and mine
the situation's very much the same.'

BOOK I.12

THE THIEVES AND THE DONKEY

Two robbers stole a donkey; then they fought.
One wished to keep it, but the other thought
    that they should put it up for sale.
    And while they battled tooth and nail
    (with self-defence their main concern),
    another rascal came; in turn
he seized poor Ned, and took his prize away.
Sometimes the parts the beast and robbers play
belong to some poor province, made the prey
of thieving princes, say in Bucharest,
or others in Stamboul or Budapest.
    That's three, and not just two, I've found:
supplies of such material abound.
It often happens that of all these thieves
none wins; another comes (and that makes four)
to take the province for himself, which leaves
the other three in harmony once more.

BOOK I.13

SIMONIDES IS SAVED BY THE GODS

The gods, the girl you love, the king: these three
   cannot be offered too much praise.
   So said Malherbe,* in former days,
   and for myself, I would agree;
   what he advised is valid still.
For praise gives much delight; it earns goodwill;
and pretty girls, when praised, have often shown
their gratitude with favours of their own.
Let's see how gods respond when gratified.
Simonides* the bard was once employed
to eulogize an athlete. Having tried,
   he found his subject bare and void.
The family's achievements?—there were none.
The father was respectable; the son
   lacked qualities of any sort,
   except for being good at sport.
The topic then was thin, its interest small.
Upon his champion the poet said
whatever he could find, then spoke instead
of Leda's sons,* showing first of all
what lustre their divine example shed
on sportsmen now; recounted every fight;
and then enumerated every site
   at which the twins had gained their glory.
Thus Castor, Pollux, and their story
took up two-thirds of what was in the ode.
   The athlete read the poem through,
then paid ten crowns, a third of what he owed;
   and for the twenty crowns still due,
Simonides, he said, had best persuade
Castor and Pollux that he should be paid.
'See if your heavenly pair will make amends.
But let's stay on good terms; please be my guest.
tonight I've asked my family and friends;

I'm sure they'll be good company—the best.
   So join the party, have some fun!'
Simonides agreed, perhaps afraid
that he might miss, besides not being paid,
some show of thanks that night for what he'd done.
   The guests arrive; they drink; they eat,
   and everyone makes merry. Then
   a servant enters, at a run:
a message for the poet. In the street,
requesting that he see them, are two men;
please can he come at once? He leaves his seat.
Among the athlete's guests no eyes are raised;
   they're all too busy with their meal.
The two men are the twins his verses praised;
and to express the gratitude they feel
they've come to give a warning not to stay:
the house will soon collapse. Their words come true;
   a pillar suddenly gives way;
   above the guests the ceiling too,
   which nothing now supports, must fall,
and down it comes, breaks every glass and plate,
   and leaves in just as bad a state
   the serving-men. But worst of all,
ensuring that Simonides would get
   full vengeance for the unpaid debt,
a beam above the athlete fell and broke
his legs in several places at a stroke.
   Of those he had invited, most
   went home as crippled as their host.
The fame of this affair spread far and wide.
   'A miracle!', the hearers cried,
and to a poet whom the gods held dear
   they gave him for his verses twice
   the sum that was till then the price.
   Young men of breeding everywhere
   outbid each other offering fees
   to celebrate their pedigrees.

Returning to my text, again I find
that we should give, to gods and all their kind,
most ample praise; and in the second place,
　　if verse is paid for, no disgrace
　　attaches to the muse; and last,
　　the poet's art should be respected.
　　The great by whom we are protected
　　are honoured for it. In the past
Olympus and Parnassus* saw each other
　　as a loyal friend and brother.

　　BOOK I.14

DEATH AND THE UNHAPPY MAN

A desperate man appealed to death each day;
he said: 'You have great beauty, Death, for me;
help me, oh Death; come soon, do not delay;
　　and from my troubles set me free.'
Death thought that granting this man's plea
was something he'd be grateful for.
He finds the house, and knocking on the door
goes in. He is revealed. 'What do I see?'
the man cries out. 'I do not want it here.
How vile its presence is! I cannot bear
　　such horror and such dread.
Leave me, oh Death; oh Death, do not come near.'

The generous Maecenas, I have read,
once wrote:* 'I'd lose an arm, be gouty, lame,
one-legged, impotent: if I have breath,
enough to stay alive, I'm happy. Death,
just keep away.'—Others will say the same.

　　BOOK I.15

The same subject was treated in a different manner by Aesop, as the next fable shows. I devised this one for a special reason that obliged me to make its meaning as general as it is. But someone* put it to me that I would have done much better to follow Aesop's original, since I had left out one of his best touches; this comment made me return to his version. We cannot go further than the Ancients: all they have left us, for our part, is the glory attached to doing well when we follow them. It is not because my fable deserves it that I have included it with Aesop's, but because it contains the remark made by Maecenas, which is so neat and so apposite that it seemed wrong to leave it out.

DEATH AND THE WOODCUTTER

A woodcutter, well on in years, and poor,
half hidden by the branches that he bore,
groaning and bent by age and by his load,
went heavily along, his footsteps slow,
toiling to reach his smoky, dark abode.
At last he stopped; further he could not go,
tired as he was, and aching from the weight.
He set his burden down. How mean a fate,
he thought, was his! Was any man on earth
worse off? What pleasures has he had since birth?
He cannot rest, and sometimes has no bread,
    yet wife and children must be fed,
    and soldiers lodged and given board,*
    and then there's tax and debts to pay,
besides the work exacted by his lord.
    In desperation, there he stood,
and called for death. Death came without delay,
and asked what he should do; is something wrong?
The man says: 'Could you help me lift this wood
    on to my back? It won't take long.'

With death our woes will go away,
but when it comes, we'd rather stay;

we have our human motto, you and I:
  better to suffer than to die.

BOOK I.16

THE MIDDLE-AGED MAN AND HIS TWO LOVES

A man of middle age, with some
  grey hairs upon his head,
decided that the time had come
  to find a wife and wed.
To pick and choose he could afford:
of cash he had a goodly hoard.
Though all the local ladies sought
to catch his eye and please his heart,
he did not hasten to be caught:
to choose aright is not a simple art.
Just two he took a fancy for,
both widows: one was young, and still
quite fresh; the other had the skill,
along with ripeness, to restore
the charms that Nature had destroyed.
Their company he much enjoyed;
they saw to it with jokes and fun,
and each of them when thus employed
would often give him a coiffure:
they did his hair. The older one,
to make him look, like her, mature,
among the hairs remaining black
each time would snip a few away.
The younger widow would attack,
in turn, the hairs already grey.
The upshot was, between these two,
quite soon their suitor lost his hair.

He saw what had occurred, and said:
'Fair ladies, all my thanks are due
for having shaved my scalp so bare;
I haven't lost, but gained instead,
since I've decided not to wed;
whichever one I took to wife,
it's she, not I, who'd run my life.
Though I am bald, you both have earned
my gratitude for what I've learned.'

BOOK I.17

THE FOX AND THE STORK

Sir Fox went to some trouble one fine day:
he offered lunch, if Madam Stork would stay.
The meal that he prepared was small
(he lived in frugal style); no meat or fish:
a thin ungarnished broth, and that was all.
He served it in a wide and shallow dish.
The lady with the long thin beak got none.
    The fox drank up, and didn't stop,
    the rascal, till the meal was done;
    he didn't leave a single drop.
In time, to take revenge for this deceit,
Dame Stork invites him: will he condescend
to visit her, and have a bite to eat?
'Of course,' he answers, 'to oblige a friend,'
and on the day he trots along the road,
most punctually, towards the stork's abode.
For her politeness he is full of praise;
the meal must surely be well cooked, he says;
above all else, his appetite is keen
(in foxes, that is what it's always been).
He was enraptured by the smell of meat,

which Mistress Stork had cut up small.
To make things awkward, though, she served this treat
inside a narrow vase: the vase was tall,
which suited well the stork's long neck;
her beak can reach right down to peck.
It's different for the fox; his snout
   can't get the tiniest morsel out.
   Back home at last he has to go,
   still hungry, with his head hung low,
his tail between his legs, as full of shame
as if he had been captured by a hen.

Deceivers, you're the target for my pen:
if you play tricks, you can expect the same.

BOOK I.18

THE BOY AND THE SCHOOLMASTER

I write because the story should be told
of one who chose a foolish time to scold.
   Upon the riverbank one day, a boy
slipped and fell in, while playing with some toy.
But providentially, just at that place,
there stood a willow, which by Heaven's grace
kept him afloat: its branches overhung
   the flowing stream; to them he clung.
The local schoolmaster was passing by;
the boy cried out: 'Please save me, or I'll drown!'
The pedagogue, approaching at his cry,
saw fit to give an ill-timed dressing-down;
he spoke in solemn tones: 'You tiresome brat,
to get into a foolish scrape like that!
Why do we have such wretches in our care?

Unhappy parents of this tiresome child,
doing their best to stop him running wild!
I feel for them—they must be in despair.'
His lecture done, he helped the boy to land.
Those whom I blame like him, a numerous band,
comprise all those who chatter, carp and preach;
they'll see themselves in what I say, and each
    makes up a tribe that grows apace;
the Lord has poured out blessings on their race.
    At any time they only seek
    an opportunity to speak.
My friend, I am in danger: save me, please;
and when I'm safe, make speeches at your ease.

BOOK I.19

THE COCK AND THE PEARL

    Scratching for food, a cock once found
    a pearl half-buried in the ground.
He took it to the jeweller down the street,
and said: 'It's very pretty, I can see,
    but still, some corn that I can eat
    is much more suitable for me.'

    An ignoramus once possessed
    a manuscript from some bequest.
He took it to a bookseller to sell,
and said: 'I know it's written very well,
    but money I can spend will be
    a lot more suitable for me.'

BOOK I.20

THE HORNETS AND THE HONEY-BEES

From what he makes the craftsman will be known.
   Some combs of honey lay neglected
till hornets came and claimed them as their own;
   this claim was by the bees rejected.
Before a certain wasp the case was tried;
he found the issue tricky to decide.
   Those bearing witness told the court
that often creatures of the flying sort
were seen around the combs, resembling bees,
quite long, with stings, and wings that made a buzz,
their bodies covered in a brownish fuzz.
   'So what?—since features just like these,'
   the hornets argued, 'would apply
to us.' To this the wasp found no reply;
   he looked for more clarification,
   arranging for the court to hear
   a nest of ants; their information
   still left the matter far from clear.
   'What use is this, I'd like to know?'
   enquired a very thoughtful bee.
   'The case began six months ago;
it hasn't moved an inch, it seems to me.
Delay will not improve the honey's taste.
   The judge should show a little haste.
   Has he not evidence enough?
   Let's put aside conflicting pleas,
   and interlocutory decrees,
   and precedents and all that stuff.
Just let us work: you'll see which side knows best
   how waxen combs are built, each cell
   with honey tasting sweet as well.'
   The hornets could not do this test;
   they lacked the skills that they would need;

which made the judge at last concede
the bees had justice on their side.

God grant that here our lawsuits might be tried
in this way too. It is the Turkish way:
no legal codes, but simple common sense—
    a method saving much expense.
Lawyers instead live well on what we pay,
dragging the cases out by long delay.
If once you go to court, the men of law
will have the oysters; you, the shells to gnaw.*

BOOK I.21

→→·❲══════❳·←←

THE OAK AND THE REED

'You should', the oak one day said to the reed,
'protest against what Nature has decreed.
    On you, the wren, a tiny weight,
    prevents your stem from standing straight.
The breeze across the lake, that in its course
will scarcely stir the water, has the force
    to make you bow your head and yield;
    whereas on high my lofty crown,
like mighty Caucasus, provides a shield
against the sun in summer beating down,
    and when the winter comes, prevails
    no less against the storm. For you,
whatever winds may blow are northern gales;
just puffs of air to me. But if you grew
    within the shelter I provide
beneath my leaves, my branches spreading wide,
you would be spared the hardships you endure,
and I would keep you, in the storms, secure.
Yet you are born within the winds' domain,

along wet shores, and there you must remain.
I think that Nature is, to you, unfair.'
'Your sympathy displays', replied the reed,
'your innate goodness. But there is no need
   to offer your concern and care,
for tempests threaten me far less than you.
I bend, and do not break. While hitherto
you have not bowed before their dreadful blast,
   we'll see what happens at the last.'
   And on the skyline, as he spoke,
the wildest of the children of the north
broke from her womb, and bursting forth
   bore down on them in rage. The oak
stands upright; the reed bends. The storm then blows
   more strongly still, and overthrows
the tree that touched the heavens with his head,
and with his feet the empire of the dead.

BOOK I.22

AGAINST THOSE OF FUSSY TASTES

Had I, at birth, been given by the muse,
the epic muse, the gifts she promises
to those who love her, even so, I'd choose
to consecrate them to the falsities
of Aesop; lies and verse have long been friends.
Whether my favour with the muse extends
to doing well in tales that Aesop told
I am not sure. Those fictions known of old
can shine anew; it can be done. I try.
Success may come to one more skilled than I.
   Already, though, my tales have shown
   how wolves might speak, and lambs reply,

  in accents hitherto unknown,
and in my fables trees and plants as well
are talking creatures.* Who then would deny
    that stories cast a magic spell?
    Some critic will appear and say:
'You're speaking in a most pretentious way
of half a dozen children's tales in rhyme.'
Your judgement, critic, seems to me severe.
But if you wish for something more sublime,
of greater gravity, I have it here.

Ten years of siege around the Trojan wall*
had tired the Greeks, who though employing all
the arts and tricks of war, and having made
attack after attack, raid after raid,
had not subdued the city or its pride,
but then created, as Minerva bid,
a wooden horse, an artifice untried
and marvellous, in which they hid,
each with his squadron, cunning Ulysses,
impulsive Ajax, brave Diomedes,
whom this colossal monster, in its flanks,
would take inside to where the Trojan ranks,
even their gods, would perish, easy prey
abandoned to the Greeks' marauding rage:
a stratagem seen in no other age,
and which by its success would soon repay
its authors' constancy and skill.

'Enough,' some author says; 'allow me, if you will,
to breathe: that sentence has outrun its course.
Those heroes in their wooden horse,
with squads of men—all that's a stranger tale
than crows and foxes and their piece of cheese.
Besides, in epic style you're not at ease.'
—All right: I'll shift it one step down the scale:*
The jealous Amaryllis thought to weep

unseen except by dog and sheep;
she moaned for false Alcippe. Tircis, though, had slid
    among some willows, where he hid;
    from there he saw the shepherdess;
    these words he heard her voice address
to Zephyr, who would bear them through the air
    gently towards her lover's ear.

My critic interrupts: 'I stop you here;
I can't allow these rhymes that you've devised:
the air together with *her lover's ear.*
    That passage ought to be revised.'
—Confound you, critics, will you never cease?
    Why can't I tell my tale in peace?
It's dangerous, attempting to provide
poems that fussy critics like to read.
You seem eternally dissatisfied;
you and your like are not a happy breed.

BOOK II.I

THE RATS WHO HELD A COUNCIL

A cat whose name was Rodilard*
made life for rats extremely hard,
and very few could still be seen,
so many had already been
by Rodilardus laid to rest.
Those living yet were much distressed;
to leave their holes they did not dare,
subsisting on the thinnest fare.
Among this wretched folk a story spread:
this Rodilard was not a cat, they said:
    he was a demon straight from hell.
One night, the lusty feline went to tell

THE RATS WHO HELD A COUNCIL

his latest conquest of his ardent love,
   and while, upon the tiles above,
   the pair embraced and caterwauled,
below a quiet conference was called,
and here the remnant of the rats discussed
the measures that might bring them some relief.
   The very prudent rodent chief
   began by saying that they must,
around the neck of Rodilard, with string,
attach a little bell, without delay,
which when the cat was hunting them would ring;
   alerted, they would run away
   into their holes and stay secure.
No other remedy would work as well.
They all agreed: it was the only cure.
   The problem was to fit the bell.
'Not me, I'm not an utter fool,' said one;
another said: 'I don't know how, I'm sure.'
The council was adjourned with nothing done.
Many a chapter meeting have I seen
of monks, not rats, assembled to consult,
which then has broken up without result:
cathedral canons also, with their dean.

At court the king debates: and all around
   advisers know the right solution;
   but when the plan needs execution
   the volunteers cannot be found.

BOOK II.2

THE TWO BULLS AND THE FROG

Two bulls were fighting for a double prize:
a heifer and a kingdom at one stroke.

A frog, observing them, heaved mournful sighs.
'Why so?' enquired another of the folk
    who croak.
    The first one answered: 'Don't you see?
The battle done, the consequence will be
that one is exiled, and obliged to yield
the rights he has across his flowered field;
no longer will he rule the grassy meads,
but here will rule our marshes and our reeds.
His hooves will crush us on the river's floor,
    first one, then two, then many more.
I tell you, ours will be a sorry plight,
and all because Miss Heifer made them fight.'

    These fears were based on common sense.
The victor forced his rival to retreat;
he hid among the frogs at their expense;
dozens were squashed each hour beneath his feet.
    Alas! the weak will always rue
    the foolish things that great ones do.

BOOK II.4

THE WOUNDED BIRD AND THE ARROW

Pierced by an arrow with its feathered flight,
wounded to death, a bird bemoaned her plight;
a thought still sharper drew from her this cry:
    'Alas! from us our ruin springs!
You cruel men, who have taken from our wings
the means to make your deadly arrows fly,
do not be scornful; think of this instead:
you share our fate, oh race without remorse;
of your destruction humans are the source;
among the children that Prometheus bred*

one half creates, and will do evermore,
weapons the other half will use in war.'

BOOK II.6

THE LION AND THE FLY

'Be off, disgusting insect, filthy pest!'
A lion in these terms one day addressed
   his comments to a biting fly,
who made a declaration, in reply,
of war. 'They call you King of Beasts,' he said;
'why should that title fill me full of dread?
Why should I care? A creature stronger still
than you are', said this gnat, 'I can control:
I make an ox go anywhere I will.'
   This speech complete, at once he blew
   the call to charge: he played the role
   of trumpeter and hero too.
Manoeuvring for advantage, drawing back,
he gets into position for attack;
   he waits his moment, then he dives;
   and on the lion's neck he drives
his enemy quite mad. The carnivore
   opens his foaming mouth to roar
with eyes aglare; and creatures terrified
   all run about and try to hide;
   the panic spreads; and all of that
   is due to action by a gnat.
The little runt attacks from every side:
on rump he bites, on muzzle too; then goes
   to bite inside the lion's nose.
And now the victim's rage has reached its height:
the unseen insect glories in the sight,
and mocks him as he tries, to no avail,

to soothe his itching flesh with tooth and claw
which only scratch and tear; his skin grows raw
    with self-inflicted wounds; his tail
resounds against his flanks; he lashes out
to beat the air, quite empty all about.
His frenzied rage fatigues him, and at length
he kneels defeated, losing all his strength.

    The insect left the battle-zone
    puffed up with triumph. Having blown
    his trumpet for attack, he blew
    for victory, and off he flew
    to tell the world. Along his way,
its web well spun, a spider lay in wait;
and there in turn the insect met his fate.

    What lessons does this tale convey?
    It seems that there are two, and first,
the smallest enemies may be the worst.
    And secondly, a man may dare
terrific dangers and emerge alive,
    who nonetheless does not survive
some everyday and trivial affair.

BOOK II.9

→→·(⇐═══⇒)·←←

THE LION AND THE RAT
THE DOVE AND THE ANT

Be kind if possible to one and all:
we often need the help of someone small.
I give you two examples I have found;
    upon this matter proofs abound.

Emerging from the earth without much thought
between a lion's claws a rat was caught.
But showing what a monarch ought to be

THE LION AND THE RAT

the King of Beasts, this time, let him go free.
He benefited from this kindly deed.
You wouldn't think a lion might have need
of what a rat could do for him, and yet
the lion at the forest's edge one day
was captured, trapped beneath a net.
For all his roaring, trapped he had to stay.
The rat returned, and chewed, till one by one
the cords were cut, and then the net undone.
Thus patience will with time at length
accomplish more than rage and strength.

    The persons in my other tale
    are creatures on a smaller scale.
A dove stood by a limpid stream to drink.
    An ant was standing there as well,
    and leaning out too far, she fell.
    She struggled but began to sink,
    her efforts vain amidst this ocean.
The dove then had a charitable notion:
into the stream she threw a blade of grass,
along which promontory the ant could pass,
    and thus she safely came to land.
Just then, barefoot, a villager walked by;
he had, by chance, a cross-bow in his hand.
The bird beloved of Venus caught his eye.
'That pigeon's just the thing', says he, 'to fill
my kitchen pot', looks forward to his meal,
and gets his cross-bow ready for the kill.
The ant, approaching, stings him on the heel.

    He turns to look. The dove has heard,
and off she flies, away into the sky.
    Supper has vanished with the bird;
that peasant won't be eating pigeon pie.

BOOK II.11 AND 12

THE ASTROLOGER IN THE WELL

There once was an astrologer who fell
    down to the bottom of a well,
and people said: 'Poor fool, you cannot tell
that something's there before your eyes;
how can you read the future in the skies?'

No more of him; but in itself his case,
for most of us who form the human race,
has much to teach. Among us, not a few
like to be told, while thinking that it's true,
that we can read the Book of Fate, and know
what will befall. However, long ago,
or so it seems from Homer and his line,
    fatality meant chance, while now,
for Christians, fate is Providence divine.
    Now, random chance does not allow
    the slightest knowledge in advance,
for if it did, you couldn't call it chance.
Is certain knowledge found in luck, in lot,
in fate or fortune?—absolutely not.
And as for Providence, what can be known
of Him who does all things, and all things right,
        except to Him alone?
His thoughts are hidden; why should we be shown,
inscribed among the stars within our sight,
his secret purpose, veiled in time's dark night?
    What use is that?—to exercise
the minds of those who study worlds and skies?
    How does it help if we suppose
we can avoid inevitable woes?
We'd be deprived of pleasure in the good
were we to know of it before we should;
a joy is lost foreseen ahead of time.
This theory's wrong; indeed, it is a crime.

The firmament revolves, the planets move;
    the sun shines on us every day;
each day it drives the shades of night away;
    and all these things will only prove
that by necessity the sun must bring
illumination to the world, must lead
the seasons round in turn, must ripen seed,
and stars must influence each earthly thing.*
Besides, how can we possibly relate
    the movements of the universe,
    invariably regular, to fate,
    so variable and so perverse?
Forgers of horoscopes, you frauds, depart,
and leave our courts and monarchs; rid us too
of all those alchemists, whose so-called art
    is no more trustworthy than you.

This outburst might have gone too far, I think.
To mention our deluded friend again,
the one who was compelled to have a drink,
not only are his methods false and vain,
he is the perfect type of one who cares
only to dream of castles built in Spain,
and puts at risk himself and his affairs.*

BOOK II.13

THE HARE AND THE FROGS

    A hare lay in his form, and mused.
What can a form be for, unless it's used
to muse? He was in deeply gloomy mood;
his fears will often make this creature brood.
Said he: 'For beings timidly inclined

THE HARE AND THE FROGS

serenity is hard to find.
They eat, but get no pleasure from their food.
Such is my life: no joys are unalloyed,
but always by some fright destroyed.
At night, bedevilled by my fears, I keep
my eyes wide open:* that is how I sleep.
"You should control yourself," I seem to hear
some wise man say; but how is fear controlled?
In fact, I think, if humans were sincere
  they also would admit to fear.'
While pondering these matters, he patrolled;
  he was a nervous, anxious hare,
  whom tiny things sufficed to scare,
  a shadow or a puff of air.
  Reflecting still upon his fears
  this beast of melancholic cast
stopped short: a little sound had reached his ears:
  the cue for going homeward fast.
He ran beside some water; as he passed,
down go the frogs: into the pool they leap,
to hide in froggy grottoes, dark and deep.
'Oho!', he said, 'what others do to me
  I've also done; I made them flee.
  As I approached them, panic spread:
throughout their ranks I caused alarm and dread.
How can I be more valiant than before?
Have I become a thunderbolt of war,
that animals should tremble where I tread?
However cowardly you are, it's clear
that even greater cowards will appear.'

BOOK II.14

THE COCK AND THE FOX

On sentry duty, in a tree, there stood
a sly old cock. A fox, with gentle voice,
addressed him thus: 'Brother, the news is good;
the war between us foxes and your race
is at an end; we are at peace; rejoice!
Come down, and leave your tree; let us embrace!
    I beg you, though, do not delay:
I've many calls like this to make today.
So go about your business, have no fear:
    it's safe henceforth for you and yours;
rely on us; we foxes will be there
        to give assistance with the chores.
    Come, celebrate; tonight, prepare
    a festive bonfire. Now descend,
    and let us two exchange a kiss,
as brothers should.' The cock replied: 'I share
your pleasure at this news of peace, dear friend—
    for what could give me greater bliss
            than news like this?
    And that these tidings come from you
    adds even more to my content.
Two greyhounds now I see; they must be sent
as messengers, to say your news is true.
    They're moving fast, and at that pace
    they'll soon be here. I'll come down too,
and all of us together can embrace.'
'Goodbye, my journey's long, I mustn't stay,'
the fox said; 'let us choose another day
to mark this great event'; and turning tail
ran off, annoyed that such a ruse could fail.
The wily cock was laughing with delight
to know the fox had suffered such a fright;

the pleasure will be doubly sweet
if you deceive the master of deceit.

BOOK II.15

THE LION WHO WENT HUNTING WITH THE ASS

A thought came to the King of Beasts one day
(it was his birthday): why not hunt for prey?
For lions, that's not sparrows: they want more—
like big fat bucks and does, and big fat boar.
To help him in his plan, the lion's choice
fell on the ass, he of Stentorian voice,
to act as hunting horn and make a din.
The lion found a bush to hide him in,
installed him at his post, and told him: 'Bray!'
The noise, so he believed, would even scare
the stoutest beasts, and drive them from their lair.
None of the animals, until that day,
had ever heard so wild a storm of sound;
the uproar burst upon the air around;
 the forest dwellers, seized by dread,
 all took to flight, and as they fled
into the waiting lion's trap they fell.
 The ass said: 'Didn't I do well?'
He wanted greater credit than his due
 because of all the noise he'd made.
'Why, yes,' the lion answered; 'bravely brayed;
did I not know your lineage and you,
 I might myself have been quite scared.'
 By this the ass was much displeased;
 he would have said so had he dared;
 and yet he had been rightly teased,

for who could leave an ass to boast unchecked?
A boastful ass is not what you expect.

BOOK II.19

AESOP'S EXPLANATION OF A WILL

W as what they say of Aesop true?
If so, he was the oracle of Greece.
I hope, dear reader, that you like this piece,
   which shows us neatly that he knew
   as much as teams of judges do;
      our Aesop was the wiser.

A father with three daughters found all three
as different from each other as could be.
The first one was a perfect miser;
the second drank; the third was a coquette.
The law demanded that a will be made;
he made a will. Each daughter was to get
one third of all he owned. A last bequest
went to their mother: she was to be paid
the same amount as they, when they possessed
no longer what they'd had from his estate.
The father died. His daughters could not wait
   to find out what they stood to gain.
They tried to understand the will: in vain.
For what could the testator's meaning be
in saying that each child, as legatee,
as soon as she no longer had her share
must pay her mother? If you have to pay,
to lack the wherewithal is not the way.
   It was a difficult affair:
   what had the father meant to say?
   The heiresses resolved to take

advice from legal experts, who,
    perused the matter, thought it through,
    and reckoning that they could make
no sense of it, confessed that they were mystified.
They merely told the sisters to divide
    the property by three, and leave
the question of a surplus on one side.
'Regarding what the widow should receive,
    the Court advises thus,' they said:
'the sisters must contract, upon request,
to pay her the amount of her bequest,
supposing that she does not want instead
    to take an income from her third
to date from when the husband's death occurred.'

To this the three agreed. They made three lots:
the first comprised his villas with their bars,*
    set out in pleasant leafy spots,
    each staffed by slaves, with wine in jars,
    and jugs and silverware galore,
    and precious vintages in store;
with everything, in sum, that one might need
    to foster drunkenness and greed.
The second lot contained accommodation
    suited rather for flirtation:
town houses elegantly furnished, where
were kept the costly gowns and jewels to wear,
coiffeurs, a resident *couturière*,
and eunuchs in attendance close at hand.
    The last lot was the farms, the land,
    the household goods and labourers' tools,
    the oxen, herdsmen, sheep and mules.
With all arranged, some nagging doubts arose:
the legatees must draw these lots; suppose
that none of them received what she preferred?
What now?—and so, with values all assessed,
the sisters simply took what pleased them best.

It was in Athens that this case occurred,
and all, both great and humble, thought it fair
      to let the sisters choose their share.
Not Aesop, though. He was the only one
to show his disagreement. He contended
that after all their trouble, they had done
the opposite of what the will intended.
'If the dead man', he said, 'could live again,
      how bitterly he would complain
against the people of this city, who
believe themselves the cleverest in the land,
      while what he wanted them to do
they absolutely failed to understand!'
This said, he redistributed each lot,
against the sisters' wishes: what they got,
      now he had changed each daughter's share,
      were things for which they did not care.
      Thus to the one who flirted went
      the bars and all the fittings meant
for drunkards; to the miser were assigned
the hairdressers and gowns; the one inclined
to wines and liquors had to be content
      with farms and sheep. This distribution,
so Aesop argued, was the one solution
to make the three do what the will required,
and give up all the wealth they had acquired.
For they would marry, when their wealth was known,
some husband wealthy too; then they could pay
their mother ready money straight away;
and since, once wed, they would no longer own
the family estate,* this would fulfil
      all the provisions of the will.

The public was amazed: could one man's mind
contain more sense than all the rest combined?

BOOK II.20

THE MILLER, HIS SON, AND THE ASS

To M. de Maucroix

By right, those born the first create the forms of art.
The ancient Greeks devised the fables that we tell;
but in that field their harvest left some little part,
and late arrivals find some gleanings there as well.
The lands of fancy still contain untrodden ground
where new resources for our writers can be found;
thence comes the clever story I recount below.
Racan was told it by Malherbe* some time ago.
These two, to Horace worthy rivals, and his heirs,
Apollo's devotees, our masters, in a word,
once met by chance where they could not be overheard,
and talked in private of their personal affairs.
Racan began as follows: 'You are of an age
to have experience of life at every stage;
you are acquainted with the world and all its ways,
and nothing, after all these years, escapes your gaze.
I must decide upon my life: what should I do?
My birth, my talents and my means are known to you.
Should I acquire a post at court, or under arms,
or lead a rural life on my estate instead?
Each situation brings both pleasures and alarms;
war has its joys, and there are dangers if we wed.
Were it for me alone, I could decide with ease,
but I have King, community and kin to please.'
Malherbe exclaimed: 'Do you expect to please each one?
Then let me tell you of the miller and his son.

This miller and his son, so I've heard tell,
the father somewhat old, the child not small,
some fifteen years of age as I recall,
once took their donkey to the fair to sell.

THE MILLER, HIS SON, AND THE ASS

To keep him fresh, he should be carried there,
they thought; he'd fetch a better price in town;
and on a pole they slung him upside down;
he hung between them like a chandelier.

"The dolts! the bumpkins! what a stupid pair!"
the first to see them said, and loudly laughed;
"the long-eared one is not the one that's daft.
Or are they acting farces at the fair?"

The miller, seeing that he looked absurd,
put down, untied and rearranged the beast,
who loudly brayed, annoyed to be released;
travel by air, he thought, he much preferred.

The miller, heedless, set the boy astride,
told him to go ahead, and followed last.
Three worthy merchants, as it happened, passed;
the sight displeased them, and the eldest cried:

"Dismount, young man, for let it not be said
you have a servant who is old and grey;
the young should let their elders lead the way."
The son got off, the father rode instead.

Three girls went past, and one called out: "For shame!
He makes his son trudge after, while he tries
to sit there like our bishop looking wise.
He looks more like a moon-calf, all the same."

"At my age, girl, there are no calves, you'll find,"
the miller said. "Now take advice from me,
and go your way." Then further repartee
went flying to and fro; he changed his mind,

and on his mount behind him placed the lad.
But barely fifty yards along the road

another group found fault. "That double load",
said one, "will kill their ass. They must be mad.

Just look at what a dreadful state he's in!
He must have served them twenty years at least:
they should take pity on the poor old beast.
No doubt they're off to town to sell his skin."

"To please the world, his wife, and everyone,"
the miller said, "I swear, is mad indeed.
Let's see if somehow, this time, we'll succeed."
So both of them dismounted, he and his son.

The donkey strolls ahead, alone, at ease.
A passerby encounters them, and says:
"Tell me, is it the fashion nowadays
for men to sweat, while beasts go as they please?

Which one, of Neddy and his master, pray,
is fitted best to labour and to serve?
Their shoes wear out, their donkey they preserve.
He should be in a shrine and on display.

They're not like Nicholas, who in the song*
went wooing on his ass, for here we find
a donkey at the front, two more behind."
"Enough," replied the miller, "I was wrong.

I've been a donkey, I confess; it's true;
henceforward, whether folk approve or chide,
come praise or blame, I'll do as I decide."
He did so, and so doing, prospered too.

Yourself, serve Mars, or Cupid, or your king at court,
reside in town or country, travel, go or stay,
get married, rule a province, join the Church; in short,
choose any course: the world will surely have its say.'

BOOK III.1

THE WOLF IN SHEPHERD'S CLOTHING

A wolf had hunted sheep from local fields,
but found the hunt was giving lower yields.
He thought to take a leaf from Reynard's book:
disguise himself by changing what he wore.
He donned a smock, and took a stick for crook;
    the shepherd's bagpipes too he bore.*
The better to accomplish his design,
    he would have wished, had he been able,
    to place upon his hat this label:
'My name is Billy and these sheep are mine.'
    His alterations now complete,
    he held the stick with two front feet;
    then pseudo-Billy gently stepped
    towards the flock, and while he crept,
    upon the grass the real Billy slept.
    His dog as well was sound asleep,
his bagpipes too, and almost all the sheep.
The fraudster let them slumber where they lay.
By altering his voice to suit his dress,
    he meant to lure the sheep away
and take them to his stronghold in the wood,
which seemed to him essential to success.
    It didn't do him any good.
He couldn't imitate the shepherd's speech;
the forest echoed with his wolfish screech.
    His secret was at once undone:
    his howling woke them, every one,
    the lad, his dog, and all his flock.
    The wolf was in a sorry plight:
amidst the uproar, hampered by his smock,
he could not run away, nor could he fight.

Some detail always catches rascals out.
    He who is a wolf in fact

THE WOLF IN SHEPHERD'S CLOTHING

like a wolf is bound to act:
of that there's not the slightest doubt.

BOOK III.3

THE FROGS WHO ASKED FOR A KING

The frogs, who had a democratic state,
grew tired of it; their clamours rose so high
that Jupiter decided to create
    a monarchy for them to try.
The king who fell among them from the sky
    was most sedate, but in his fall
    made such a splash that, one and all,
    this breed of creatures who reside
    in bog and marsh, a silly breed,
    and very timid, ran to hide:
    they hid in rushes, beds of reed,
in muddy pools, or anywhere they could.
They stayed for hours, afraid to go too near:
they thought it was some giant lying there.
    In fact it was a block of wood.
The first to venture out was greatly scared,
it looked so solemn; but, still trembling, dared
approach his king. Another did the same;
a third; and then in multitudes they came.
They grew familiar, and then much bolder;
they even climbed upon their monarch's shoulder.
    A kindly sire, he never stirred,
    and didn't say a single word.
Soon Jove was plagued by protests, as before:
'We want our king', they said, 'to do much more.'
The lord of high Olympus sent a crane,
    who pecked them, killed them, pecked again,

THE FROGS WHO ASKED FOR A KING

and ate them as he wanted at his leisure;
   which made the frogs once more complain.
Said Jove: 'And is it following your pleasure
   that I, the King of Gods, must reign?
   Why did you change, in any case,
   the government you had in place?
   You asked me for a king: I sent
a quiet one, which should have made you glad.
With this one now, you'd better be content;
   the next one might be twice as bad.'

BOOK III.4

THE FOX AND THE GOAT

Commander Fox was travelling one day.
His friend the goat was with him on the way.
   Although his horns were very tall,
   the billy goat was one of those
   who cannot see beyond their nose.
The fox was full of tricks: he knew them all.
They found an open cistern; needing drink,
they jumped right down, and both most amply drank.
The fox remarked: 'My friend, we've quenched our thirst,
   but there's a problem: can you think
   how we might leave this water tank?
If you stand upright on your hind legs first,
   then press your horns against the wall,
you'll be just like a ladder; then I'll crawl
along your back; your horns will make a ledge:
if I can stand on them, I'll reach the edge,
and when I'm out, I'll see you get out too.'
'Well, by my beard, that is a brilliant scheme,'
   the goat exclaimed; 'I much esteem

those people who have brains like you.
I never would have thought of that, I know.'
The fox climbed out. He left the goat below,
and urged on him, in pious exhortation,
the need for patience. 'If at your creation
    the Lord had given you', he said,
'as much by way of sense inside your head
    as you have hairs upon your chin,
you might have thought before you jumped in there.
    And now, goodbye; I'm out, you're in.
Try to escape; try hard, and persevere.
There's something I must do elsewhere,
    which stops me staying here with you.'

In everything, it's best to keep the end in view.

BOOK III.5

THE GOUT AND THE SPIDER

Hell having made the spider and the gout
addressed them thus: 'My daughters: do not doubt
that you are both, which is no little boast,
amongst the things that humans fear the most.
Let us consider where you should reside.
I offer you a hovel, meanly built;
or else a splendid palace bright with gilt.
Choose one to live in; if you can't decide,
draw lots: here are two straws, one long, one short.'
'A hovel? I'll have nothing of the sort,'
replied the spider. But the gout's position
was not the same, for palaces employed
too many of the species called physician;
she thought that they were buildings to avoid:

The hovel seems the better place to go.
She takes up residence upon the toe
of a poor man, and spreads herself at ease.
   'I don't believe', she says, 'that here
    I'll waste my time; nor need I fear
that any student of Hippocrates*
will make me pack my bags and go elsewhere.'
Meanwhile a chamber richly lined with wood
becomes the spider's home. She settles in
   as if she meant to stay for good,
and had a lifetime lease; she starts to spin:
stretches her web, catches her prey.
   A servant comes to sweep the room,
    and breaks the web with busy broom.
Another web is spun; it's swept away.
The wretched beast is forced to move each day.
At last, her efforts proving vain, she went
to see the gout; who having had to ride
backwards and forwards through the countryside
   was also full of discontent.
   Her sufferings have been severe:
much worse than any spider had to bear.
Her host had carried her upon his toe
   when he was digging up a field,
    or working with his axe or hoe.
You need to knock your gout about a bit,
they say; just give a shake, you'll soon be healed.
'Sister,' she gasps, 'I cannot suffer it;
   I'd like to try your palace, please.'
   The other one at once agrees;
    into the poor man's hut she creeps,
and stays. There are no brooms, and no one sweeps.
   The gout, inside the palace, goes
    to find a foot on which to perch,
belonging to a pillar of the church,
whom she condemns to stay in bed. God knows
   how many poultices he had;

for people's conduct is perverse,
and when they're faced with something bad
they're not ashamed to make it worse.
The gout and spider's lot was much improved;
they acted wisely when they moved.

BOOK III.8

THE WOLF AND THE STORK

All wolves are gluttons when they eat;
and one, when feasting on his meat,
gobbled the lot, they say, so fast,
he very nearly breathed his last.
A bone lodged in his throat and stuck;
he couldn't call for help, but had some luck:
he saw a stork, who at the signs he made
flew down to offer him her aid.
She operated on him with her beak.
She took the bone out with a tweak;
the wolf had life and breath restored;
the stork requested some reward.
'Reward, my dear old dame?' he said;
'to ask for more is quite absurd:
I let you take away your head
although I had it in my jaws.
Be off with you, ungrateful bird;
in future, mind my teeth and claws.'

BOOK III.9

THE LION DEFEATED BY A MAN

There was a picture once displayed
in which the artist had portrayed
a giant lion, which one man alone
        had fought and overthrown.
As viewers basked in their reflected glory
a passing lion quelled their boastful chat.
'You won,' he told them, 'in this painter's story;
he tricked you, though, when he invented that.
An artist is permitted some pretence.
        But we would have defeated you,
which after all is only common sense,
        if lions painted pictures too.'

BOOK III.10

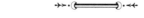

THE FOX AND THE GRAPES

A fox from Gascony, some say,
from Normandy,* say others; either way,
a fox half-starving, saw above his head
some grapes upon a trellis; deepest red,
they were quite clearly ripe and sweet.
Gladly would he have had them to devour,
but couldn't reach. He said: 'They are too sour;
fit only for some rustic clown to eat.'
        And that was better, I maintain,
        than had he chosen to complain.

BOOK III.11

THE LION IN OLD AGE

The lion whom the forest saw with dread
mourned his lost power; age had bowed his head.
By those he ruled he was attacked at length,
they growing stronger from his lack of strength.
    The horse was first to dare his den,
and kicked him; next the wolf, who bit; and then
    the ox, who gored him with his horn.
    The wretched lion, weak, forlorn,
can scarcely roar; with age he's lost his breath.
    Without complaint, he waits for death,
but when, approaching him, he sees the ass:
'This is', he says, 'too much to bear, alas!
Though death is welcome, being struck by you
    is not one death alone, but two.'

BOOK III.14

THE DROWNED WOMAN

This phrase, unlike some men, I won't employ:
'No matter; just some woman drowning.' No:
I say it matters greatly. Men should show
much grief for women, since they are our joy.
These comments seem gratuitous, no doubt,
but lead to what this fable is about:
a woman's miserable fate; her life
was ended in a river when she drowned.
    Now since the corpse could not be found
the husband started searching for his wife,
to bury her with honour in the ground.
Some people walking at the river's side

whence came such sorrow when she died
were ignorant of what had just occurred,
and so, when asked if they had seen or heard
something to help him find her, one replied:
'No, nothing; but the current surely took
the corpse downstream; and that's where you should look.'
    Another man broke in to say:
'It's not; you ought to search the other way.
However steep the river's course downhill,
    however fast the current flows,
with feminine contrariness she will
float back against the way the water goes.'
His joke was neither tactful nor polite.
Regarding awkwardness of mind,
    I do not know that he was right;
but whether women are, or not, inclined
    towards a failing of this kind,
whoever is possessed of it at birth
    remains with it till laid in earth;
    they contradict until they die,
    and even after that they try.

BOOK III.16

THE CAT AND AN OLD RAT

A cat—so says an author I have read—
was Rodilard* reborn: for other cats
their Alexander, and a scourge to rats,
a Genghis Khan for them; the life they led
was miserable. My author says as well
he truly was a cat sent out of hell,
for he was bent on the extermination
    of all the rodent population.
For miles around, they trembled at his name;

THE CAT AND AN OLD RAT

the cheese we put in traps, the poisoned bait,
those planks which tip beneath the mouse's weight—
such things, compared to him, were just a game.
But now that neither rat nor mouse would dare
      to quit the safety of its lair,
and nowhere were his victims to be found,
      the cunning feline made it seem
      that he was dead: beneath a beam,
head down, a yard above the ground,
he hung suspended, but the naughty thing
      held himself up by means of string.
'It's punishment,' said all the rats and mice.
      'Perhaps he stole some meat or fish?
      or scratched a face, or broke a dish?—
but anyway the brute has paid the price:
he's dead.' In unanimity they swear
they'll go to watch his funeral and cheer.
Then rodent noses show at holes; they peep,
and then retreat; a step outside they creep,
then venture forth in quest of food to eat.
But what is this? The corpse has come alive;
      drops down on them on all four feet;
      amongst the laggards few survive.
      'An ancient stratagem of war,'
he says, and starts to eat; 'I've many more.
Don't think you're safe there, skulking down below;
where these are going, others too will go.'
He told them true: to get them in his power,
this gentle puss, one day, employed some flour
to whiten fur and whiskers; thus disguised
he went to find the flour-box at the mill,
      then crept inside and stood stock still.
It did its work, this trick that he'd devised:
the creatures of the small and scurrying kind
went sniffing round to see what they could find,
      and came to grief. Just one refrained;
this rat was old, and knew a thing or two,

a veteran, he'd long campaigned;
his tail was missing, bitten through.
  'There's something wrong, you lump of white,'
he shouted over to the cat-in-chief,
while keeping out of reach; 'it's my belief
that it's some trick; that flour does not look right.
  So even if you're just a sack
  you won't catch me; I'll stay well back.'

To me, his comments seem both right and just:
for by experience this rat had learned
that safety and security are earned
by practising suspicion and mistrust.

BOOK III.18

THE LION IN LOVE

To Mademoiselle de Sévigné*

My lady, whom the Graces choose
to be their model on this earth,
  who brought us beauty from your birth,
I hope, though love's a passion you refuse,
you'll like this story, since it means no harm;
but can you contemplate without alarm
  a lion forced by love to yield?
  Strange is the force that love can wield;
  better from tales alone to know
  how deep the wounds it makes can go.
  If those who talk of love to you
  offend, though what they say is true,
  you may at least, I think, be told
  of love in stories: this makes bold
  to offer you, once more renewed,
  devout respect and gratitude.

Long, long ago, when animals could speak,
the lions (mainly; others too) would seek
alliances by marriage with our race.
Why should they not?—the race of lions then,
for sense and courage, equalled that of men.
   Besides, they had that handsome face.
   On one occasion, this took place:
   a lion born of high degree
   while by a meadow chanced to see
   a shepherd maid. She was, he thought,
   the kind of girl he'd always sought.
   He asked her father for her hand.
   A husband causing fear and dread
   was not the one the father planned.
   It seemed unkind to let them wed,
   but then, if he refused instead,
   would that be safe? It might give scope
   for thwarted lovers to elope.
   He knew the girl had always been
   attached to those of lofty mien;
   and women often don't disdain
   a lover with a flowing mane.
   In consequence he felt afraid
   to tell this lover plainly: 'No.'
   He said: 'Remember that the maid
   is delicately formed, and so,
   when you embrace her, you might cause
   some damage to her with your claws.
   Permit us therefore in each paw
   to clip them short, and in each jaw
   to file your teeth less sharp, for this
   will take the roughness from your kiss,
regarding which the maid feels much concern.
She'll kiss you much more warmly in return;
   her fondness will increase your bliss.'
   And in his blindness, all intent
   on love, the lion gave consent.

With blunted teeth, with claws cut short,
he looked like some dismantled fort.
They set the dogs on him; though strong,
he did not hold them off for long.

Oh love, oh love, the world well knows:
when you have caught us, prudence goes.

BOOK IV.I

THE SHEPHERD AND THE SEA

A neighbour of the goddess of the deep*
lived free of care on earnings from his sheep,
content with what he had, which to be sure
was modest, though it was at least secure.
He liked to watch the ships return to land,
    unloading treasures on the strand.
They tempted him; at last he sold his flock,
and traded all the money on the main;
he lost it when the vessel struck a rock.
The trader went to tend the flocks again,
not as the owner that he used to be,
when sheep of his had grazed beside the sea;
not Corydon or Tircis* as before,
    just Peterkin and nothing more.
In time he had enough, from what he gained,
to buy some of the creatures clad in fleece.
And then, when winds blew gentle and restrained,
to let the ships unload their goods in peace,
    this shepherd could be heard to say:
    'You want our money, Madam Sea;
    apply to someone else, I pray,
for on my faith, you're getting none from me.'

THE SHEPHERD AND THE SEA

This is no idle tale that I invent;
it is the truth that I have told,
which through experience is meant
to show you that a coin you hold
is worth a dozen that you hope to see;
that with their place and rank men must agree;
that thousands would do better to ignore
the counsels of ambition and the sea,
or else they suffer; one perhaps may thrive.
The oceans promise miracles and more,
but if you trust them, storms and thieves arrive.

BOOK IV.2

THE GARDENER AND HIS LORD

A villager, not middle class, though more
than just a peasant, once possessed
a cottage garden with the plot next door;
and gardening was what this man loved best.
He planted hedges, and a fine array
of lettuce, sorrel, and some flowers too
to make, on Margot's birthday, her bouquet;
there scented thyme and Spanish jasmine grew.
A hare disturbed this gardener's content.
Complaining, to the local lord he went.*
'At dusk and dawn each day, this wretched hare
gets through the hedge,' he said, 'and has a feast.
No sticks or stones affect him in the least;
    he simply laughs at any snare.
He must be a magician in disguise.'
'Magicians I defy,' the lord replies;
'were he Old Nick himself, my Nimrod here
will hunt him down, whatever tricks he tries.

I'll see you're rid of him, good man, I swear.'
'Can you come soon?'—'Tomorrow: why delay?'
And so it was agreed. He came next day;
his men came with him. 'First,' he said, 'let's eat;
those chickens there are tender, I daresay.
Was that the daughter of the house I saw?
Let's see you, miss: come here, we ought to meet.
When is the wedding? Where's the son-in-law?
Good man, that means big bills, you understand:
dig deep; your purse-strings won't stay tied.'
He greets the pretty girl and takes her hand,
then takes her arm to seat her at his side,
then tries to lift the scarf around her neck:
these fooleries the girl, with due respect,
    makes efforts all the time to check,
the father, meanwhile, starting to suspect.
But in the kitchen now the cooking's done;
    the place at once is overrun.
    'Those hams of yours are looking good;
    when were they cured?' 'Sir, if you would,
accept them; they are yours.' 'Indeed? Why then,'
the lord replies, 'most readily, I will.'
He and his entourage all eat their fill,
    his dogs, his horses and his men,
    with good strong teeth to help them dine.
He gives commands as if he owned the place,
    does as he pleases, drinks the wine;
the girl he gets into a close embrace.
Their meal complete, the hunters surge around;
    in much commotion all prepare;
the din of horns and shouting fills the air;
the householder is deafened by the sound.
Still worse the havoc that they wreak
    across the poor man's kitchen plot:
each tiled path is wrecked, each boarded bed;
goodbye to chicory, goodbye to leek,
goodbye to everything that fills his pot.

The hare lay by a giant cabbage head.
They find the scent; he starts, he makes a dash
and finds a hole—no, not a hole: a gash,
a gap that in the hedge the men had made,
   because their lord must be obeyed,
   and he had said it would not do,
   when someone's hedge was in the way,
if gentlemen could not go riding through.
The poor man said: 'Like royalty at play',*
but no one paid attention. In an hour
the men and horses did more damage there
than hares throughout the country in a year.

Take care, you princes who have little power,
between yourselves to settle any scores.
   To put your quarrels in the hands
of mighty kings is madness. In your wars
don't ask their help; and keep them off your lands.

    BOOK IV.4

THE BATTLE OF THE WEASELS AND THE RATS

The members of the weasel race
   in common with the cats
have never shown the least goodwill
   towards the race of rats.
If rats lived anywhere except
   in holes with tiny doors
the long-backed creature would, I think,
   have slaughtered them in scores.
One year when rats were populous,
   their king, called Ratador,
prepared an army, well equipped,

and sent it into war.
The weasels also raised their flag.
    Historians relate
that fighting lasted many hours
    and victory came late.
In many squadrons gaps appeared,
    and bloodstains soaked the land;
but everywhere the greatest loss
    fell on the rodent band.
The rats were wholly overwhelmed;
    their army fled pell-mell.
Though Psicrapax, Medyrapax,
    and Artrapax as well,
their bodies covered by the dust,
    had managed to maintain
a stout defence against the foe,
    their efforts proved in vain.
To fate they had to yield at last.
    When troops and captains tried
to look for shelter somewhere safe,
    the officers all died.
The rabble had no trouble, since
    in making their escape
they had their ratholes ready-made
    adjusted to their shape.
But splendid plumes, or horns, or crests,
    adorned each captain's head,
whether to indicate their rank,
    or fill the foe with dread.
It brought about their doom, because
    no hole would let them pass,
no crack nor nook nor chink, unlike
    the rats of lower class;
for these the smallest gap sufficed.
    Among those left to lie
the highest numbers were, therefore,
    the rats whose rank was high.

It often hampers you to wear
    a helmet with a plume;
proceeding proudly with a crest
    requires a lot of room.
At any awkward time, when things
    have reached a parlous state,
the lesser folk escape with ease;
    it's harder for the great.

BOOK IV.6

THE APE AND THE DOLPHIN

By voyagers of ancient Greece
    a custom was maintained:
to take on board a dog or ape
    that fairground men had trained.
While bearing these to Athens once
    a vessel ran aground.
Without some dolphins who were near
    the humans would have drowned.
These creatures are great friends to men,
    the elder Pliny said;
and in his writings I believe
    whatever I have read.
The dolphins rescued all they could;
    one even helped an ape,
to whom it was a benefit
    to be of human shape.
This dolphin took him for a man
    because he looked the same;
he rode to shore like Arion,*
    whose singing won him fame.

THE APE AND THE DOLPHIN

The dolphin asked the ape by chance
   when nearly at the coast:
'Is mighty Athens where you live?'
   'Yes: there I'm known to most.
If you have problems, let me help;
   my relatives in Greece
are highly placed; my cousin is
   a sergeant of police.'
The dolphin thanked him; then he said:
   'Piraeus* too must see
Your Honour's presence there, no doubt?
   You visit often?'—'He',
the ape said, 'is my oldest friend;
   I see him every day.'
He wrongly thought the port a man,
   and gave himself away.
And there are many who, like him,
   take Vaugirard* for Rome;
they prate about the whole wide world,
   when all they know is home.
The dolphin laughed, and turned, and saw
   the beast he'd helped escape:
he'd rescued from the deep blue sea
   merely a grinning ape.
Throwing him back, away he sped
to save a human in his stead.

BOOK IV.7

THE WOLF, THE NANNY-GOAT, AND HER KID
THE WOLF, THE MOTHER, AND HER CHILD

A goat in need of grass, her udders dry,
   went out to find a fresh supply,
   but first made sure the door was barred.

She told her kid: 'Keep careful guard;
for Heaven's sake let no one in,
unless, to show they're friends, they say
"Down with the Wolf and all his kin!"'
But as she spoke, the beast of prey
by chance walked past and overheard.
He duly noted every word.
The mother, as you surely guessed,
had not observed the glutton there.
She left; and when his way was clear,
he asked to enter, did his best
to change his voice and sound sincere,
and in an unctuous tone he cried:
'Down with the wolf!' He had no doubt
that straightaway he'd get inside.
Behind the keyhole, peeping out,
the kid suspiciously replied:
'First show me that your paws are white,
or else you won't come through this door.'
On wolves (you may have heard before)
white paws are not a common sight.
This one, outwitted by the kid's reply,
returned the way he'd come, unfed.
What would have happened if, instead,
the kid decided to rely
on passwords that the wolf, by chance, had learned?
Where safety measures are concerned,
you're better off with two than one;
precautions can't be overdone.

This wolf's mishap has brought to mind
another creature of his kind
who was more thoroughly caught out:
he died; and here is how it came about.

There was a villager's abode
some little distance from the road.

Outside the gate Sir Wolf would prowl
in case some happy chance befell;
he'd seen fat lambs there, unweaned calves as well,
and regiments of guinea-fowl—
good eating of all sorts, in brief.
That day a lengthy wait had bored the thief,
but then he heard a youngster howl.
At once the mother starts to scold:
unless he stops, the boy is told,
she'll give him to the wolf to eat.
Thanking his gods, the wolf, with joy,
looks forward to this unexpected treat;
but now, to soothe the bawling boy,
the mother tells her darling: 'Dry your tears;
we'll kill the beast if he appears.'
'What's this?' exclaims the murderer of sheep;
'you made a promise that you ought to keep.
How do you dare behave like that
to personages such as me?
D'you take me for a fool? Just let your brat
come out to gather cobnuts—then we'll see!'
But scarcely were the words pronounced
than men came from the house; a guard-dog pounced,
and staves and pitch-forks held the wolf at bay.
And what, they asked him, was he looking for?
He tells them what he heard the mother say.
'Well, thanks,' she says; 'you'd eat the child I bore?
He wasn't made to give some wolf a feast.'
They slaughtered the unlucky beast.
A churl cut off his feet and head,
which then the squire put up for show
upon the manor wall; he wrote below
this local proverb which can still be read:
'Good Maister Wolf, art but a fool
to trust in mothers' words when childern mewl.'

BOOK IV.15 AND 16

THE MISER WHO LOST HIS TREASURE

Possession comes from use, and use alone.
I ask, of those whose passion is to own,
who heap their money up, then more, then more,
what gains do misers garner from their store
that others lack? Diogenes,* no doubt,
in Hades, is as rich as they are here;
like his, their lives are beggarly and poor.
A man whose treasure Aesop knew about
will serve as my example, as you'll hear.
A second life this wretch would have required
in order to enjoy what he'd acquired
without possessing it: he was possessed.
His treasure, buried, lay inside its nest,
and there his heart lay too; his sole delight
was ruminating on it day and night.
    He made of it a thing divine;
if he was going, coming, eating, drinking,
you would be lucky not to catch him thinking
about the treasure lying in its shrine.
Too often did he go to where it lay;
a gravedigger observed him, looked around,
suspected something precious underground,
and took the booty secretly away.
Next day the miser found the nest was bare.
He wept, he moaned, he heaved pathetic sighs;
    he beat his head and tore his hair.
A man came past, and asked him: 'Why these cries?'
'My treasure has been stolen.' 'Stolen? Where?'
    'I kept it buried by this boulder here.'
    'Out here? Why bring it all this way?
Is there a war on? Better let it stay
at home, in private, under lock and key,
not take it somewhere else. You would be free
to spend it when you wanted, at your ease.'

THE MISER WHO LOST HIS TREASURE

'To spend it? Gods! Is that what you suggest?
Once gone, it's gone: it doesn't grow on trees.
I never touched it.' 'Tell me, in that case,'
the other answered, 'why you're so distressed.
If this was money that you would not touch,
    just put that boulder in its place:
    to you it will be worth as much.'

BOOK IV.20

THE MASTER'S EYE

A stag escaped the hunt and fled inside ·
    a stable where some oxen stood.
        Observing him, they said: 'You should
        look for a better place to hide.'
'Do not betray me, brothers,' he replied;
'I'll teach you something you'll be glad to know:
the meadows where the sweetest grasses grow;
perhaps you'll find it valuable one day.'
The oxen promised silence, come what may.
He breathed again, took courage and revived.
Near evening, the stable lads arrived.
They brought some forage and fresh hay;
they went about their duties, to and fro;
the foreman did as well; and did they see
    the branching pointed antlers? No:
they saw no stag. The forest refugee
remained, waiting for when he could depart:
when all the others leave to do the tasks
    that Ceres for her service asks.
        Meanwhile he thanked them from his heart.
'So far,' a ruminating ox replies,
'so good; but he who has a hundred eyes

has not yet done his rounds. Should he appear,
on your behalf, poor stag, I feel great fear.
Unless he's come and gone, you can't relax.'
At which the master enters to inspect.
'What's this—there's not much fodder in these racks,'
he says. 'It's old, this bedding on the floor.
Your beasts ought not to suffer such neglect.
Off to the granary, and bring some more.
Those corners full of spiders should be swept.
I want those yokes and halters neatly kept.'
He saw a head, while looking everywhere,
unlike the heads that usually were there.
The stag was recognized; with hunting spears
they stabbed the beast; he died, despite his tears.*
The corpse went to be salted and preserved;
of meals it gave a plentiful supply;
and many joyful neighbours too were served.

    As Phaedrus elegantly says:
No keener glance than from the master's eye.
To which I'd add, myself, the lover's gaze.

BOOK IV.21

THE SKYLARK AND HER YOUNG, AND
THE OWNER OF A FIELD

    Rely on none, the saying goes,
except yourself; what it might mean
a tale I take from Aesop shows.

    In cornfields, when the corn is green,
the skylark nests, around the time of year
when all things love and flourish, far and near:
aquatic monsters, in the deep concealed;

THE SKYLARK AND HER YOUNG

in forests, tigers; skylarks in a field.
   One of the latter sort had let
the weeks and months slip past, and had not yet
tasted the joys that love in spring will yield.
At last, however, she resolved one day
     to follow nature, come what may,
     and start once more on motherhood.
     Then hastily, as best she could,
     she built a nest, began to lay,
     sat on the eggs and hatched them out.
But now the ripening corn stood all about,
and with her fledgling chicks too weak as yet
to leave the ground and fly, the lark, beset
by anxious thoughts, must search for food.
Before she goes she tells her little brood
to stay alert, and always keep good guard.
'Now when the field's owner, with his son,
comes here (as he is bound to), listen hard,'
she says, 'for much depends on what you hear.
We may all have to leave our nest and run.'
As soon as she has left her family there
     the owner and his son appear.
Says he: 'It's ripe for cutting, is this corn.
Go round and see our friends, and ask each one
to bring his sickle here tomorrow morn,
at break of day, to get the reaping done.'
     The skylark finds, on her return,
     among her nestlings, much concern.
'Mother, his friends are coming', one began,
'at dawn tomorrow to help, said that man.'
     'If that is all you overheard,
we need not rush,' replied the mother bird;
'No need just yet to pack our things and go.
Attend to what he says tomorrow, though.
I've brought your food; cheer up and eat your fill.'
They eat, then fall asleep, and all is still.
The dawn arrives: no sign of any friends.

Into the sky the lark ascends;
below, the owner does his usual round,
observes the corn ungathered in the ground,
    and says: 'This corn has stood too long.
    Our friends are wrong to be so slow
    in giving help, and we were wrong
to count on sluggards. Son, you'd better go
around our kinsfolk with the same request.'
This causes consternation in the nest.
'He said his kinsfolk—surely, mother, they . . .'
'No, no, my children—we'll stay here just the same.
    We shall not have to move today.'
    The lark was right, for no one came.
The owner for the third day running paid
a visit to his field of corn. 'We made',
he said, 'a bad mistake when we relied
on help from others. Son, you should depend
upon yourself, not relative or friend:
remember this. And now, we must decide
on what's the quickest way to get things done.
Tomorrow, with our household, every one,
we'll bring our sickles here and make a start.
We'll get the harvest finished when we can.'
The lark, as soon as she had heard this plan,
said: 'Children, now it's time; we must depart.'
And silently the nestlings, that same day,
fluttering, jostling, tripping, crept away.

BOOK IV.22

THE WOODCUTTER AND MERCURY

To M. L. C. D. B.*

Upon your principles my works are based,
my lord: my method is to please your taste.
Elaborate adornment you reject,
nor do you favour straining for effect.
The work is spoiled when authors try too hard.
You ban grandiloquence, and I do too;
it's not that subtler touches should be barred:
I like them, and they much appeal to you.
As for what Aesop tells us is his aim,*
I stumble on towards it, and would claim
that though perhaps our goal is out of reach
I try at least to entertain and teach.
    I cannot boast that I belong
among those heroes famed for being strong;
    my fables seek to combat vice
    by turning it to scorn; I lack
the might of Hercules for my attack.
Whether my gifts, such as they are, suffice,
    is not, I think, for me to say.
My stories for example are replete
with envy joined to foolish self-conceit,
twin poles round which our lives revolve today,
    as in the puny beast who tries
      to match the ox for size.
The contrasts which my work presents,
virtue and vice, good sense and lack of sense,
the lamb, the ravening wolf, the ant, the fly,*
    in double images supply
an ample comedy, its scenes diverse:
so many that they span our universe.
Both gods and men, and creatures large and small,
appear in them; I have a role for all,
including Jove. But let me introduce

the lesser god he sends, as go-between,*
to beauties whom he wishes to seduce.
That's not the subject of my latest scene.

A woodman lost his livelihood,
his axe; he vainly searched the wood,
and wept in pitiful despair.
It's not a tool that he can spare;
he has just one: all else he lacks.
Mine is, he thinks, a hopeless case,
and as the tears run down his face:
'My axe! oh my beloved axe!'
he cries; 'oh Jupiter, restore
this axe to me; I shall once more
owe you my life.' His plaintive cry
was heard by Jupiter on high,
and Mercury arrived. 'I may
have come across your axe near by,'
the god declared; 'so can you say
which one of these might be your own?'
An axe of solid gold was shown;
the woodman told him: 'That's no good.'
A silver axe was next in line:
refused. Then iron blade on wood:
'You've found it!' he exclaimed; 'that's mine!
A wooden handle does for me.'
'You'll have them,' said the god, 'all three;
your honesty deserves reward.'
'Why then, if so,' the woodman said,
'I'll take all three.' His story spread
throughout the woods; with one accord
the forest lads who chop and hack
all found they'd lost their axes too;
they shouted loud to have them back.
As he observed the noisy queue,
the great god Jupiter, in doubt
which one to help, sent down his son.

to each in turn, the god held out
another golden axe; each one,
reflecting that he'd be a fool
if he refused to take it, said:
'It's mine!'—and Mercury, instead
of giving him the golden tool,
used it to beat him round the head.

With what you have already, be content.
Be truthful too: that's best; and yet, intent
on getting more, we practise our deceits—
in vain: for Jove cannot be tricked by cheats.

BOOK V.I

THE POT OF IRON AND THE POT OF CLAY

Talking with the Pot of Clay,
Pot of Iron asked him whether
they might take a walk together.
Pot of Clay declined: he'd stay;
best to sit beside the fire.
Walking might be a mistake:
little bumps could make him break;
just the one it would require;
into pieces he would crack.
'You', he said, 'should not stay in;
yours is much the tougher skin.'
Said his comrade: 'You'll get back
safe and sound; for if some rock,
or some other thing that's hard,
threatens you, I'll be your guard,
saving you from any shock.'
Pot of Clay accepts this plan.

Two pots stagger down the street,
lurch along as best they can,
three legs each and side by side;
every obstacle they meet
makes them stumble and collide.
The pot of clay was very soon undone:
almost before the journey had begun
the pot of iron broke him, and he lay
    in fragments strewn along the way.
Nor did he have occasion to protest;
when choosing our companions, it is best
to stay with equals. Otherwise, I fear,
    our fate may be what happened here.

BOOK V.2

THE FISHERMAN AND THE LITTLE FISH

A little fish will bigger grow
if Heaven lets it live; but even so
to set one free, and wait until it's fat,
then try again: I see no sense in that;
I doubt that it will let itself be caught.

An angler at the river's edge one day
had hooked a carp. 'A tiddler still,' he thought,
but then reflected, looking at his prey:
'Well, every little helps to make a meal,
    perhaps a banquet; in the creel
    is where you'll go, to start my store.'
    As best it could, the fish replied:
'What kind of meal d'you think that I'll provide?
I'd make you half a mouthful, not much more.
I'll grow much bigger if you throw me back;

THE FISHERMAN AND THE LITTLE FISH

then catch me later on; I'd fill a sack.
A full-grown carp's a fish that you can sell;
some greedy businessman will pay you well.
　　But now, you'd need a hundred fish
the size that I am now, to fill a single dish.
Besides, what sort of dish? Hardly a feast.'
　　'No feast? quite so,' replied the man;
　　'it's something, though, at least.
You prate as well as parsons can,
my little friend; but though you talk a lot
this evening it's the frying-pan for you.'

A bird in the hand, as they say, is worth two
in the bush; the first one is certain, the others are not.

BOOK V.3

THE PLOUGHMAN AND HIS CHILDREN

No fortune brings more certain gains
　　than working hard and taking pains.
A ploughman who had prospered from his land,
　　aware that death was near at hand,
summoned his sons and spoke to them alone.
'Let no one buy', he said, 'the land we own.
Our forebears passed it on; and in that field,
but where I know not, treasure lies concealed.
You'll have to look for it, and to succeed
　　a firm resolve is all you'll need.
Take plough and spade and pick; begin
　　as soon as all the harvest's in,
and turn the soil; let not a yard remain
unless it has been dug and dug again.'

The father died; the children tilled the ground
across and up and down, throughout. They found
no buried treasure; but, next year, the soil
grew more and better crops.—That man is wise
    who shows his sons before he dies
    that treasure is the same as toil.

BOOK V.9

THE MOUNTAIN THAT GAVE BIRTH

In labour pains, a mountain groaned so loud
that all the people gathered in a crowd,
believing, as they heard her piercing cries,
    the child would be, without a doubt,
a town to rival Paris by its size:
    and at the birth, a mouse came out.

        Considering this fable,
which through the lies it tells is able
    also to tell us truth, I find
the image of an author* in my mind;
says he: 'Those arms I sing that Titans bore
against the God of Thunder making war.'
To me this sounds a promising affair;
    what do we get? Hot air.

BOOK V.10

THE DOCTORS

THE DOCTORS

A patient who was seeing Doctor Fearful
was also visited by Doctor Cheerful.
The latter hoped to cure him, while his rival
did not expect the sufferer's survival.
Each had a cure on which he was relying.
The patient chose what Fearful had suggested,
    but then paid Nature's debt* by dying.
    The death, each doctor still protested,
showed he alone was right. 'For I could tell
he'd soon be dead,' declared the fearful one.
'But if what I advised him had been done,'
the other said, 'he'd be alive and well.'

BOOK V.12

THE HEN THAT LAID THE EGGS OF GOLD

Wanting it all will lose it all,
and avarice does that. So let me call,
to give some evidence for what I say,
on him who owned a chicken who would lay
    (or so in fable we are told)
        a golden egg each day.
Deciding that inside her she must hold
        a treasure-house of gold,
he killed her, opened her, and found the same
as in the hens from which no riches came.
He had destroyed the jewel of his store.

    Those people always seeking more
    can learn a lesson from this dunce.

THE HEN THAT LAID THE EGGS OF GOLD

How many of them recently have passed
from wealthy man to pauper all at once
    because they wanted wealth too fast!

BOOK V.13

THE SNAKE AND THE FILE

A snake, the story goes, once lived next door
    to where a clockmaker resided
    (for him, a neighbour to abhor).
Into his shop one day this serpent glided,
    and needing food to fill its craw,
    it searched around but only saw
a steel file which it began to gnaw.
    The file, which kept its temper, said:
'Misguided thing, what can you hope to do?
    You've tackled stuff too tough for you.
    Poor little snake with empty head,
    before you've managed to obtain
    the smallest fraction of a grain
    of steel from me, your teeth will crack.
I am immune to all but time's attack.'

To you I speak, you worst of those who write,
who good for nothing only seek to bite,
an aim that it is futile to pursue;
    great works that you attack will feel
no damage from your teeth: they are for you
as hard as diamonds, or bronze, or steel.

BOOK V.16

THE BEAR AND THE TWO FRIENDS

Two friends, hard up for money, sold
a bearskin to a furrier they knew.
  The bear was still alive, it's true;
they'd kill it soon, the furrier was told.
Of all bears known, they said, this one was king,
  and large the profit it would bring;
    the skin so big that it would form
two coats, not one, and keep the wearers warm
    in any frost or freezing storm.
The salesman Dindenault,* with sheep to sell,
could not have advertised them half as well
as they did with their bear. (I call him theirs—
    that's their opinion, not the bear's.)
Delivering the goods, they said, would need
two days at most. A contract was agreed.
They started on their search; and met the bear,
    approaching briskly at a trot.
The two were thunderstruck; beset by fear,
    they broke their contract on the spot,
but neither said: 'There's compensation due:
    the bear's the one we'll have to sue';
    the first had just sufficient time
    to run towards a tree and climb;
the other, cold as ice, fell to the ground.
He held his breath, pretending to be dead,
    because, somewhere, he'd heard it said
that if a body which a bear has found
seems not to live, or breathe, or move, the bear
will often not attack, but leave it there.
This bear was tricked, the fool; he should have known.
    He sees the body lying prone,
believes it lifeless, but suspects a snare,
so nuzzles it and rolls it to and fro,

then sniffs to check the passageways of air.
'Smells bad,' he says. 'A corpse; I think I'll go.'
He wanders off towards the woods nearby.
    The merchant who was perched on high
      descends to see his friend and say
that it's a miracle, to get away
    with just a nasty fright. 'But how',
he asks, 'd'you think we'll get our bearskin now?
And did he whisper something in your ear?
I saw him pawing you—he put his head
right next to yours.' The friend replied: 'He said:
"Don't sell the skin until you've killed the bear."'

BOOK V.20

THE DONKEY CLAD IN THE SKIN OF A LION

    A donkey who was in
      a lion's skin
once gave the neighbourhood a fright.
    This quadruped who cannot fight
brought terror to the people all about.
But then he had bad luck: one ear stuck out;
they saw that he'd misled them with a trick.
    So Martin-Cudgel* raised his stick,
      and struck the donkey such a clout
he ran back to his mill,* and double-quick,
    while those who had not heard the news
    about this donkey's naughty ruse
    were very much surprised to see
    how Martin made a lion flee.

Many in France are cheered and clapped
    for whom this allegory is apt.

Without the warlike costumes they put on,
three-quarters of their valour would be gone.

BOOK V.21

THE SHEPHERD AND THE LION
THE LION AND THE HUNTSMAN

In fable, things are not as they appear:
the animals become our teachers there.
Though lessons bore us when they're bare and plain,
in narrative they pass: the tale enthrals.
Such fictions must both teach and entertain;
narration for narration's sake soon palls.
Authors of note for reasons such as these
have written fables to instruct and please.
The pompous and the prolix they eschew;
they never use two words where one will do.
Phaedrus was blamed for being too concise;
for Aesop, even fewer words suffice.
Another Greek composed more curtly still:
in Spartan style, both elegant and terse,*
each tale comprised a mere four lines of verse.
Let experts judge if he did well or ill.
　　To show you how the two compare
I'll take a theme that he and Aesop share.
One fable has a huntsman, one some sheep.
The ending and the incidents I keep,
but add a few small touches on the way.
Here is what Aesop says in his account.

A shepherd, looking at his sheep one day,
　　saw fewer than the rightful count.
　　He swore the thief would be detected.

He went to where a wolf might go to ground
that was the breed of villain he suspected—
    to spread some traps for wolves around.
    Before he left, he knelt in prayer:
'Oh King of Gods, grant me the pleasure of redress:
could I but see this rascal in my snare,
    the fattest calf that I possess
    I'll sacrifice to you.' Just then
appeared a mighty lion from his den.
Half-dead from fright, the shepherd ran to hide.
'How blind is man to what he wants!' he cried;
'Oh Jove, oh King of Gods, to you I said
that if I saw the thief who kills my flocks,
caught here before me in the traps I spread,
    you'd have a calf; but now I say
    I offer you a full-grown ox
if you will make this lion go away.'

Thus wrote the man to whom we owe the most;
    let us compare the one who followed.

A lover of the hunt, inclined to boast,
    believed a lion might have swallowed
a dog that he had lost, of high descent.
He met a shepherd. 'Where does he reside,'
he asked, 'this lion? Show me: my intent
is vengeance for my hound.' The man replied:
'You'll find his lair upon that mountainside.
    Each month I pay him as a fee
    one sheep in tribute; then I'm free
to wander through the meadows as I please,
without disturbance.' As they talk, they see
the lion coming from beneath some trees,
    approaching them on agile feet.
    The braggart turns to run away;
    'Oh Jupiter,' he cries, 'I pray,
    just let me find a safe retreat.'

The only test of courage worth the name
is present danger; some we see who claim
to face it down, but when it is in sight
   they change their tune and take to flight.

BOOK VI.I AND 2

THE COCKEREL, THE CAT, AND THE
LITTLE MOUSE

A youthful mouse, whose ignorance was great,
   through ignorance was nearly caught.
Back home, he had this story to relate:
'Mother, I scaled the heights around this state,
   and trotted as a rodent ought
   as he embarks on his career.
   I soon observed, as I came near,
   two animals I'd never seen:
the first one gentle, gracious, and serene,
the other turbulent and full of noise,
   its voice a shrill and raucous cry,
   with reddish flesh upon its head.
It has two arms of sorts, which it employs
   to lift itself as if to fly;
its tail is feathery, and widely spread.'
It was a cockerel, you understand,
this creature that the little mouse portrayed
as if it came from some exotic land.
'Beating its arms against its sides, it made
so great a din,' he said, 'and such a sight,
that I who, God be praised, can boast
that as a mouse I am as brave as most,
   took to my heels for very fright,
   and as I went I roundly cursed:
the brute had stopped me on my way to meet

the creature whom I'd seen at first,
whose nature seemed so kind and sweet.
His coat is patterned, but like ours is sleek;
his tail is long; his countenance is meek.
He has a modest look, but gleaming eyes.
I think that he must truly sympathize
with all of us who are of rodent race,
because his ears resemble ours in shape.
Just as I went to see him face to face,
the other's noise burst out; because of that
   I thought it better to escape.'
'My son, that gentle creature is a cat.
He wears a hypocrite's disguise,'
the mother said; 'to us and all our kind
   he is most evilly inclined.
   The other one, contrariwise,
   so far from causing us disquiet,
may one day furnish scraps towards our diet;
   by contrast, mice have always been
   the staple of the cat's cuisine.
Remember all your life that other creatures
ought never to be judged on outward features.'

BOOK VI.5

THE HARE AND THE TORTOISE

To run is not enough to win:
what counts is whether you begin
on time. Consider the affair
between the tortoise and the hare.

'I'll race you, hare,' the tortoise said;
'I bet I cross the line ahead.'
'Ahead of me?' replied the lighter beast.

'You're quite insane, my worthy friend.
   A purge is what I recommend:
   four grains of hellebore, at least.'*
'I meant it though, the wager that I made,
insane or not.' And so it was agreed.
Beside the winning post their stakes were laid;
how much they stood to win, by whom and how
   the contest would be refereed—
   such questions don't concern us now.
   Our hare could win in just four bounds,
the leaps he makes outstretched, ahead of hounds,
   and leaves them trailing on their way
   across the moors in hope of prey
on some remote tomorrow. So the hare,
believing that he had some time to spare
   to graze at leisure, take his ease
   and listen to the passing breeze,
   allowed the tortoise to proceed,
who set off statesmanlike, and with much strain
he hastened; but his haste was slow indeed.
His rival treats the contest with disdain:
what glory, when he wins, will he obtain?
   He thought his honour would depend
on starting late. He took a rest, he browsed,
he did all sorts of things except attend
to winning. Then the tortoise had to go
a few more steps. At last the hare was roused;
he started like an arrow from a bow,
as quick as lightning: vainly; for his run
   had come too late; the tortoise won.
'I told you, hare,' he said; 'although you're fast,
   it didn't help: you came in last.
   And where, I wonder, would you be
if you were carrying a house, like me?'

BOOK VI.10

THE VILLAGER AND THE SNAKE

THE VILLAGER AND THE SNAKE

A villager, so Aesop says, possessed
a charitable heart, but was not blessed
with much by way of wisdom. Once he found,
in winter, walking through his family field,
a serpent lying on the snowy ground,
its body stiff and numb, its blood congealed,
a snake from which the life had nearly fled;
within a quarter-hour it would be dead.
The peasant took it back to his abode,
    and there, not giving any heed
to how it might repay the debt it owed
    for such a charitable deed,
he laid it at the fireside, in the warm,
to heat it and revive its frozen form.
    No sooner did it feel the fire
    than life returned, but also spite;
it reared its head, it hissed, and rising higher,
it coiled its body back to leap and bite
its saviour, its benefactor too,
indeed its father; who responded: 'Fie!
If this is how I am repaid by you,
    ungrateful creature, you will die.'
So speaking, in his righteous wrath he takes
    his hatchet in his hand and chops;
    by slicing twice he makes three snakes:
    a head, a middle and a tail.
    The serpent now in sections hops
and tries to reunite; to no avail:
    it couldn't make a single joint.

Though charity is good, the point
is who deserves it. Ingrates, every one,
will die in sorrow when their days are done.

BOOK VI.13

THE SICK LION AND THE FOX

The King of Beasts an order gave
while lying sick inside his cave:
ambassadors must be assigned
by vassals of each sort and kind
to visit in his hour of need;
for envoys and attendants both
safe conduct would be guaranteed
by passports sealed with royal oath
and flowing signature beneath—
protection valuable indeed
against sharp claws, against sharp teeth.
So as His Majesty decreed
envoys arrived from every breed
except the foxes: they remained
at home. One of them explained:
'Those who have visited the invalid,
to show their loyalty in this affair,
left footprints in the dust; in every case
they point in one direction: to his lair.
Of those who have returned we see no trace.
This gives us reason to suspect.
We thank him for his passports, which, if used,
would give protection, I expect,
but ask His Majesty to be excused.
I see that many went inside his den,
but not that any have come out again.'

BOOK VI.14

THE DOG WHO GAVE UP THE SUBSTANCE
FOR THE SHADOW

In this base world, we take the false for true.
The number of the foolish, who pursue
the shadow for the substance, must amount
  to more than anyone could count.
  To Aesop's tale they ought to be directed—
the one about a dog who had a bone.
He crossed a stream and saw the bone reflected,
and jumping in to get it, dropped his own.
He nearly drowned: the water grew quite rough.
He struggled on, and paddled far enough
  to get to safety, whereupon
  he found both bone and image gone.

BOOK VI.18

THE YOUNG WIDOW

A husband's death will always cause some sighing,
but consolation comes, despite the crying,
for time has wings to bear our griefs away;
  with time our pleasures reappear.
Between the woman widowed for a day
and one who has been widowed for a year
the difference is great; you'd never guess
they are the same; the former, all men shun;
they find the other full of charm and fun.
The new bereaved will feel or feign distress;
one theme is hers, one constant protestation:
  nothing can bring her consolation,
  or so she tells us; nonetheless

this tale, or rather truth, will show
that what she tells us isn't so.

A man departing from this earthly life
was leaving too his young and lovely wife,
and at his deathbed: 'Wait for me!' she cried;
 'I will not stay here long alone;
my soul aspires to travel at your side.'
The husband made the journey on his own.
The lady's father was a man of sense.
He let things be until the storms were past,
and then, to soothe her, said at last:
'My dear, the tears you weep are too intense.
 For you to drown that pretty face
 is no advantage to the dead.
Reflect upon those living still instead.
It's not that better things must now replace
your widowed state, or that you soon must change
 your widow's weeds for wedding white;
 but in due course I'd think it right
 that you permit me to arrange
to bring a suitor whom you might espouse:
he's young, well-built, good-looking; not the least
 does he resemble the deceased.'
 'Alas!' she said, 'my only vows
will be inside a convent, as a nun.'
Her father left her nursing her distress
for one more month. She spent another one
in making changes every day: in dress,
in linen, hair, or hat; it seemed that black
was chosen not to mourn, but to adorn,
till pretty clothes could once again be worn.
 Then to the dovecote flocking back
came Cupid's lovebirds; laughter was reborn,
 the Fount of Youth* resumed its play,
while games and dancing lasted night and day.
 No longer did the father fear

the buried husband, once so dear,
but held his tongue. 'And where', his daughter said,
'is that young man you promised I should wed?'

BOOK VI.21

THE ANIMALS SICK OF THE PLAGUE

An evil that induces dread,
a scourge that Heaven in its wrath devised
that crimes on earth should not go unchastised,
the plague (would that its name were never said!),
which in a day makes rich the Stygian shore,
attacked the animals as if in war.
Not all were dying; none remained exempt.
They could not make the effort to obtain
    the means to nourish and sustain
a life now fading, which no food could tempt.
Nor wolf nor fox would lie in wait to slay
    the innocent and gentle prey.
In solitude lived every turtle-dove;
there was no joy because there was no love.
The lion called them to his council. 'Friends,'
he said, 'these woes that Heaven has permitted
are due, no doubt, to sins we have committed.
So let us sacrifice, to make amends,
the guiltiest among us. His reward,
perhaps, is that our health will be restored.
From history we learn that immolation
often occurs in such a situation.
So therefore let us all examine here
our consciences; and let us be severe.
Myself, in appetite, I've been a glutton:

I have consumed a large amount of mutton,
   although, against myself, I knew
those sheep had not committed any crimes.
It's also happened that I've had, at times,
    the shepherd too.
I'll be your sacrifice, then, if I must,
but each, I think, should do the same as I,
and say how he has sinned; for it is just
that he who bears the greatest guilt should die.'
The fox said: 'Sir, you are too good a king,
Your Majesty; in all that you confess
   you take your scruples to excess.
To eat a sheep, a slavish, stupid thing,
is that a sin? Of course not; sheep should feel
much honoured to be taken for your meal.
As for the shepherd, let it be observed
that he received no more than he deserved,
like all his kind, who baselessly declare
that they should rule, while we obey their laws.'
Thus spoke the fox, receiving much applause
from all the flatterers. They did not dare
to scrutinize too deeply any deed,
however bad, committed by some breed
   such as the tiger or the bear,
or any of the greater powers there;
the creatures of the more pugnacious sort,
down to the mastiff dogs, were one and all
as pure as saints, they said around the court.
The donkey's turn arrived. 'I chanced to pass',
he said, 'an abbey meadow; I recall
that with my hunger, and the tender grass,
the opportunity, and, it may be,
   some devil also tempting me,
I couldn't help but take a little bite.
I must admit I didn't have the right.'
His words at once provoked a hue and cry.
A wolf with claims to learning spoke, and said

this mangy, scurvy brute, from whom had spread
the dire disease, accursed beast, must die.
His peccadillo was, they all agreed,
a capital offence. For shame!—to feed
on someone else's grass? A wicked deed:
   only his death could make it good.
   They made quite sure he understood.

At court, if you are weak, you're in the wrong;
you're always right, at court, if you are strong.

BOOK VII.I

THE MAN WHO MARRIED BADLY

If beautiful were always found with good,
I'd seek a wife tomorrow, so I would;
   excuse me, though: it's nothing new
   to see divorce between these two.
Beauty in body, beauty in the soul
are seldom found together. On the whole,
therefore, that quest is one I won't pursue.
Of all the marriages that I have seen
   —and they are many—none has been
enticing; yet, among the human race,
   nine out of ten at least consent
to risk the greatest hazard they could face;
   nine out of ten of us repent.
As with the husband here; he felt remorse,
and finally found only one recourse:
   it was to banish from the house
his mean, bad-tempered, jealous spouse.
For her, the household could do nothing right:
they slept for half the day and all the night;
this work was bad, that also, and the next.
The servants were enraged, the master vexed.

Monsieur himself, she said, had overspent;
he never knew where all the money went;
and either he was always rushing out,
   or when at home, asleep no doubt.
So finally Monsieur had had enough
of being scolded by a tongue so rough;
   off to her family she was sent,
   deep in the countryside, which meant
some new companions; now her time was spent
with certain Nans and Megs, the girls who guard
   the turkeys in the poultry-yard,
and friends of theirs who give the pigs their swill.
And when it seemed she'd had the time to learn,
and might be speaking now in tones less shrill,
   the husband let his wife return.
'What did you do? How were your days employed?
And was the innocence of country life
a pleasure for you?'—'Well,' replied the wife,
'there was one thing that made me feel annoyed:
the staff were worse than here, they always shirked—
the beasts they had to tend were much neglected.
Of course, I told them how they should have worked,
and when I did, those lazybones objected.'
'Your tongue is sharp, Madame,' Monsieur replied.
'You scolded those whose time with you was brief,
before and after all their work outside;
if they could not endure to hear you chide,
what will my servants do, with no relief
from living in the house where you reside?
What will the husband do, when day and night
   you won't allow him out of sight?
Off to your village once again; farewell;
and if I'm ever tempted, and decide
to call you back, then for my sins, in hell,
may I have two like you, one either side!'

BOOK VII.2

THE RAT WHO RETIRED FROM WORLDLY LIFE

From legends that Levantines tell* we learn
   about a rat whose chief concern,
for he was weary of the life profane,
was to retire, away from stress and strain.
It was a cheese from Holland that he found;
the solitude extended all around
and consequently was profound.
Our new recluse remained in this retreat;
   he made a hole with teeth and feet,
   his hermitage was soon complete.
   He thus procured both bed and board,
   and who can ask for more than that?
   He steadily grew large and fat;
great benefits are given by the Lord
to those who hear his calling and obey.
Now to this hermit's door there came one day,
   to ask him for a small donation,
   some envoys from the tribe of rats.
A foreign country is their destination,
they need its help against the tribe of cats.
   Ratopolis is under siege, they say;
there was no money they could bring away;
   blockaded by opposing forces,
the city is deprived of all resources.
It's little that they ask; the help they seek,
there is no doubt, will come within a week.
The solitary says: 'This world's affairs,
my friends, do not affect me any more.
   Except by offering his prayers,
how can a mere recluse, alone and poor,
   assist you? All that I can do
   is hope that Heaven grants you aid.'
   With these remarks, shutting his door,
   the saintly personage withdrew.

What figure, do you think, might be portrayed
behind the selfish rat that you have seen?
A monk?—Of course not, no.—A dervish* then;
for monks, you must agree, have never been
uncharitable to their fellow-men.

BOOK VII.3

THE HERON
THE GIRL

With long thin beak, long neck, and long of shank,
a heron walked along a river bank
to nowhere in particular. Below,
the stream, as only on the finest days,
flowed past transparent to his gaze;
    there Madam Carp swam to and fro
    in twists and turns with Master Pike.
They would have made, for him, an easy feast:
the fish were close, he only had to strike.
    He thought, however, that he'd wait
    until his appetite increased;
    he had a dietary regime,
    which fixed the hours at which he ate.
    Time passed; his appetite improved.
    He saw, as he approached the stream,
some tench emerging from their reedy bed.
It was a fish of which he disapproved;
he thought he should be better fed.
This heron was disdainful, and in that
was like the Latin poet's fussy rat.*
'What! me, a heron, dine on tench?' he said.
    'I surely cannot be expected
to face such paltry fare.' The tench rejected,
he found some gudgeon. 'Gudgeon? Heaven knows,

herons should not be offered those.
Open my beak for tiddlers? God forbid!'
    But later, open it he did,
and for much less. He searched to no avail:
as it turned out, no fish were to be had;
and growing hungry, he was more than glad
    when finally he found a snail.

We should not be so delicate of taste.
The wisest take whatever may befall;
in seeking more, our chances go to waste.
Treat nothing with disdain, and least of all
when what you find will suit you more or less.
A lot of people have been caught that way,
not only herons; what these fables say
is not for birds; it's humans I address.
Another tale will show you how and why
the lessons that I give you, you supply.

A girl was somewhat haughtily inclined,
and looking for a husband had in mind
    a young one, handsome, dark and tall;
agreeable in manner; most of all
(note this) not cold, nor jealous. For the rest,
    he should be wealthy and well-bred,
    well-educated and well-read,
well everything, in brief; but who is blessed
with everything? Still, Fortune did her best.
Distinguished suitors visited the house.
Milady thought they were a feeble lot.
'What, them? Am I supposed to be the spouse
of one of those poor creatures? Surely not—
it's nonsense. That would be a dreadful fate!
    They really are a sorry sight.'
For one, she thought, was quite devoid of tact,
another had a nose which wasn't straight;
whatever wasn't wrong was not quite right.

She was a précieuse,* in fact,
and précieuses have standards to maintain;
she liked to curl her lip and show disdain.
    The eligible men departed;
some new contenders for the prize appeared.
More ordinary folk they were; she jeered.
    'Now am I not indeed kind-hearted
to let such people near? Do they assume
that I am anxious not to live alone?
Thanks be to God I have a single room,
and there I sleep in comfort on my own.'
These sentiments increased her satisfaction;
    but age diminished her attraction.
    She found herself no longer wooed.
    She spent a year in anxious mood;
    another passed, and brought dismay.
Enjoyment, love and laughter, every day,
are vanishing around her. She can tell
that now her looks have withered, and repel.
She tries cosmetics: they bring no relief;
too much is lost to Time, the master thief.
    A ruined house can be repaired;
    why can't this privilege be shared,
and ruined faces made as good as new?
Our précieuse was forced to change her tune.
Her mirror told her: 'Get a husband soon',
and certain inner yearnings said it too,
to which a précieuse is not immune.
    The choice she made, as it turned out,
    was one you'd never have believed;
    she was delighted and relieved
    to wed an ugly, shambling lout.

BOOK VII.4

THE WISHES

In Mogul lands a kind of sprite is seen
who like a household servant does the chores.
He cares for house and carriage, keeps them clean,
    and sometimes also out of doors
he does the garden. Where a sprite has been,
keep out: their work is ruined if you touch.
Beside the Ganges once, there was one such
who gardened for a man who hadn't much:
a bare sufficiency. He tilled the ground
most skilfully, this sprite, without a sound.
He loved the master and the mistress there;
the garden even more. To keep it clear,
the zephyr winds, I'm sure (good friends to sprites),
would offer help, although he did not shirk:
    the sprite was constantly at work,
to please his masters with some new delights.
Despite the fickle nature of his race,
his zeal to serve this couple was so great
he would have stayed forever in his place,
but other sprites approached their head of state,
and brought such influence to bear
that he, from whim or policy, agreed
    to send our sprite to work elsewhere;
    to Norway, so it was decreed,
    to distant Lappland he must go,
to tend a household always deep in snow.
The Hindu sprite became a Lapp instead.
    Before he left his hosts, he said:
'I have to leave you soon. I cannot say
    what it might be that I did wrong;
but go I must. I am allowed to stay
    a little while; it won't be long:
a month; perhaps a week; which you can use

to make three wishes. Anything you choose
I can produce; but just three times, no more.'
To wish is not, for men, a painful task,
　　nor one they've never done before,
　　and first of all this couple ask
for affluence. So Affluence appears,
　　and open-handed with her bears
　　much more in wine, in grain, in gold,
than cellar, granary, or safe can hold.
The place fills up until it overflows;
but how can they arrange it? Neither knows:
　　it takes such trouble, time and care;
complete bewilderment consumes the pair.
　　From robber gangs they suffered theft,
　　and noble lordships came to borrow,
　　and they were taxed on what was left:
　　what they had gained, poor things, was sorrow.
'Enough of wealth', they cried, 'that brings unease!
Of treasure rather let us be bereft
than owners of possessions such as these.
Is not the life of poverty more blessed?
　　Away, you riches! riches, hence!
And you, oh goddess, mother of good sense,
　　come back, companion of our rest,
Sufficiency, come quickly.' Whereupon
Sufficiency returns to take her place;
they're friends again; she doesn't need much space.
So there they were, this pair, two wishes gone,
from which they had received as small returns
as all who wish and wish and are content
to dream away the time that should be spent
in managing their everyday concerns.
By this misfortune both were much amused:
they laughed; the sprite as well. His offer, though,
　　was one that could not be refused,
　　and just before he had to go
　　their third and final wish was used

to ask for wisdom: which is treasure, yes,
but also not a nuisance to possess.

BOOK VII.5

THE COACH AND THE FLY

An awkward, steeply rising, sand-filled track;
   a coach that six strong horses haul.
They pant and sweat, and scarcely move at all.
The sun beats down. Unsheltered, at the back,
all walk: old men, a monk, the women too.
And then a fly arrives to see what he can do:
descends upon the horses, flits around
to get them going with his buzzing sound;
   decides it would be just the thing
     to pick on one or two to sting;
   reposes on the shafts, then goes
     to settle on the coachman's nose.
Eventually the convoy starts to stir,
and everyone gets moving; in his view
   to him is all the honour due.
Now here, now there he darts, as if he were
an officer in battle dashing round
to urge his soldiers on and win some ground.
In such a general crisis, is it fair,
he asks, that he alone should do his share?
Nobody helps the horses in their plight.
The monk is praying: that won't put things right;
   and if that woman with her song
   believes that it will help, she's wrong.
Then he himself flies round their heads and sings,
   and does some other useless things.
At last the coach completes its painful climb.

'I've done it,' says the fly; 'we've reached the plain.
    Now, horses, you can breathe again,
    and pay me for my work and time.'

    Thus busybodies everywhere
    intrude on us and interfere,
    and everywhere they are a pest:
    to send them on their way is best.

BOOK VII.9

THE MILKMAID AND THE CAN OF MILK

To market, with her milk-can firmly set
upon her head, well cushioned, went Perrette;
    she meant to get to town that day
    without encumbrance or delay.
Nimble, and lightly clad, along she strode;
    to move more quickly on the road
    short skirt and low-heeled shoes she wore.
Accoutred thus, she counted up, in thought,
the sum her milk would fetch; with that she bought
    some half a gross of eggs or more.
She's diligent, and with her careful touch
her hens hatch out three times the usual clutch.
    'It isn't difficult to raise
    more hens around our house,' she says;
'Reynard will be a crafty fox indeed
if he can take more chickens than I need
    to earn enough to buy a pig.
He'll fatten up with just some bran in mash.
Already when I bought him he was big;
    I'll sell him on for lots of cash.
Then what's to stop me having, after all,

considering the price I'll get,
a cow and calf? I'll keep them in our stall;
outside I'll watch him as he jumps about.'
At which, transported by the thought, Perrette
jumps too: the can falls down, the milk spills out.
To calf and cow, to pig, to chicks, farewell;
the mistress of these riches, now upset,
    watching her fortune disappear,
goes home to see her husband and to tell
what happened to the milk she had to sell;
    she risks a beating when she's there.
    The story of Perrette became
a fairground farce; *The Milkmaid* is its name.*

Who has not strayed in fantasy's domain,
nor built a castle for himself in Spain?
My milkmaid; Pyrrhus; Picrocole:*
we all, the foolish and the wise, adore
our waking dreams; nothing delights us more.
A flattering delusion fills the soul;
whatever men may covet, we possess;
money is ours, or women, or success.
    I challenge, when I am alone,
the bravest of the brave; across the seas
I cast the Sultan from his throne with ease.
    I have a kingdom of my own:
    my people love me; on my brow
    the diadems pour down like rain.
Some mishap brings me back to earth, and now
    I'm Johnny Lumpkin once again.

BOOK VII.9

THE CURÉ AND THE DEAD MAN

A dead man sadly made his way
towards the dwelling that would be his last;
    a curé gladly made his way
    to get the dead man buried fast.
His transport was a carriage, nothing less,
and fitting was the costume that he wore,
since 'coffin' is, alas!, the name it bore:
his summer, winter, spring, and autumn dress;
    a corpse has nothing else to wear.
    The priest who walked beside the bier
    was following the usual rite;
    with much devoutness did he pray,
    did psalms and homilies recite,
    did verses with responses say.
'Leave it to us, Sir Corpse, let us provide.
Whatever you may want can be supplied;
your lordship only has to meet the cost.'
Chouart* the curé gloated as he prayed;
keenly he watched his corpse, as if afraid
    that all this treasure might be lost.
It was a speaking look he had. 'From you,
departed lord, I'll have a tidy sum;
from that some candles for my church will come;
    some other little items too.'
    He reckoned on a year's supply
    of vintage wine, the region's best;
a niece of his,* who liked to be well dressed,
would have a new chemise; he'd also buy
another for his chambermaid Pâquette.
But while he mused upon this pleasant thought
there came a sudden bump: a wheel was caught;
and with its corpse the carriage was upset.
Monsieur le curé Jean Chouart was hit;
    the coffin struck his skull, which split.

The lord parishioner, deceased,
took off with him the parish priest;
Chouart the curé followed on
to join his lord where he had gone;
they went together on their way.

We all, in truth, are every day
this curé, counting what the corpse would pay;
Perrette* as well, the milkmaid in the play.

BOOK VII.10

THE TWO COCKS

Two cocks together lived a peaceful life.
A hen appeared, and with her, instant strife.
By love was Troy destroyed; love was the source
of that envenomed quarrelling which stained
    Scamander's current in its course
    where wounded gods themselves had bled.*
Between our cocks the fight was long maintained.
About the neighbourhood the tidings spread;
    coquettes adorned with ruddy crest
    flocked round to watch, and more than one,
among these feathered Helens fair of breast,
    were prizes for the cock that won.
The loser disappeared. He went to hide,
    and in seclusion wept and sighed:
of love, of glory was he dispossessed,
that love which now the victor, full of pride,
    triumphantly each day caressed
    before the rival's eyes. Defeated,
he regularly saw this scene repeated.
    Again his rage and courage grew.

He sharpened up his beak with care;
    against his flanks, against the air
he flapped his wings; against the winds that blew
    he exercised to make them strong;
with jealous wrath he armed himself anew;
and had no need of all that he had done.
The victor on a roof one day in song
was crowing once again that he had won.
    A vulture heard him from above:
    farewell to glory and to love;
the vulture ate him and his pride as well.
Thus by a twist of fate the victor fell,
    and soon his rival, coming back,
before his lady strutted and displayed.
    Of wives for him there was no lack;
    and what a din their cackling made!

The victor who is boastful to excess
invites defeat by trumpeting success:
Fortune enjoys these tricks. We should beware,
and having won a battle, still take care.

BOOK VII.12

THE SOOTHSAYERS

A general opinion may at base
depend on chance, but fashion will depend
upon opinion, and in every case.
These introductory remarks extend
to one and all, of high or low condition:
for everywhere there's superstition,
    prejudice and blind tradition;
    little commonsense or none.

It is a torrent: what is to be done?
   You cannot stop the torrent's flow;
   it was and always will be so.
In Paris once a Sibyl plied her trade.
To her, on all occasions, people ran along;
were ribbons lost, romantic conquests made,
if women thought a husband lived too long,
if wives were jealous, mothers hard to bear,*
then all would ask the soothsayer for aid:
they thought she'd tell them what they wished to hear.
It was her artfulness that made her art:
some hocus-pocus, many daring guesses,
some lucky chances, all had played their part.
Though no more learned than a loaf of bread,
she often had miraculous successes;
she was an oracle, the public said.
An attic was this oracle's domain.
With fortune-telling as her sole resource
   she filled her purse, and in due course
   had earned sufficient to obtain
   a public office for her spouse:
of higher rank, she moved: she bought a house.
The woman in the attic now, though new,
is treated by the public as before.
Young girls and women, lords and lackeys queue
to ask her what the future holds in store.
This attic is the Sibyl's den, it's clear:
the other woman's customers came here.
In vain the new one argues, makes her plea:
'Don't mock me, sirs! A fortune-teller, me?
My ABC was all I ever learned;
I cannot even read.' It was no good:
a soothsayer, a seer she had to be;
   gold coins despite herself she earned,
as much as any brace of lawyers could.
The décor helped, where clients were concerned:
   some rickety old chairs, a broom;

these fittings seemed the proper means
for witches' rides and transformation scenes.
Had she foretold the truth in some rich room,
with tapestries that hung along the wall,
they wouldn't have believed in her at all.
The attic was in fashion, and well-known.
Its former tenant languished on her own.

The shop-sign draws the customers inside.
    Around the law-courts once I spied
a badly fitting gown; it earned large fees;
for in its wearer people thought they saw
great Such-and-Such, whom juniors heard with awe.
    Explain the situation, please.

BOOK VII.14

THE CAT, THE WEASEL, AND THE
LITTLE RABBIT

The palace of young Rabbit, one fine day,
was seized by Madam Weasel. Full of guile,
she moved her household gods* the easy way,
the owner being absent for a while.
That morning, he was where the wild thyme grew,
paying his court to dawn amidst the dew.
Young Johnny nibbled, trotted round,
did all his errands, went to graze some more,
then back to his abode beneath the ground.
Dame Weasel poked her nose outside the door.
'Ye gods hospitable, what's this about?'
    exclaimed the rabbit now expelled
    from land his ancestors had held.
'Dame Weasel, you're not wanted here; get out:
just quickly take your things and go.

If not, the local rats* will want to know.'
   The lady with the pointed nose
replied that rights of ownership arose
from present occupation; furthermore
this hole was surely not a cause for war:
      it was so small
that he himself, to enter, had to crawl.
'Were it a king's estate, I do not see',
she said, 'that there is any law at all
   which says the owner has to be
some John, the son or grandson of some Paul,
   but never James, nor Charles, nor me.'
John Rabbit argued, to support his cause,
from custom and tradition. 'By their laws
I am the lord and master of this place,'
he answered her; 'by them it was passed on
through generations of the rabbit race,
to Peter, Simon, and to me, young John.
Are laws of occupation any stronger?'
   'Enough of this,' the weasel said.
   'No need to squabble any longer:
we'll ask Grimalkin to decide instead.'
This cat was one affecting saintly ways,
a canting cat, smooth-tongued, benign of gaze,
   with fine thick fur, and sleek and fat;
no judge more skilled in law had ever sat.
Young John agreed that he should hear their case.
   They went together to appear
before his furry worship, face to face.
He said: 'Come closer, little friends, just here;
   I'm deaf; it is old age, no doubt.'
The two approached: they saw no cause to fear.
And when the pair were both within his reach,
the hypocrite Grimalkin, stretching out
   his two front paws, caught one with each;
the arbitrator settled their dispute
by eating both the parties to the suit.

This brings to mind the outcome that awaits
when little kings appeal to mighty states.

BOOK VII.15

DEATH AND THE DYING MAN

Death does not take the wise man by surprise.
Always prepared to take his leave and go,
    he has already learned to know
    when he must confront his own demise;
    and that can be at any time at all.
Divide your life by seconds, hours, or days:
at each, alas! may come the fatal call
to pay the tribute every creature pays.
The moment when a prince first sees the light
    may also sometimes be the same
that sends him on his journey into night.
Defend yourself by rank, or try to claim
that death should spare your beauty, virtue, youth:
he plunders everything, he has no shame.
The whole world will one day enrich his store.
There's nothing we know better than this truth,
and nothing we try harder to ignore.

A man had lived a hundred years or more,
and now that he was dying, he complained.
Why such a hurry? Why was he constrained
to leave so soon? He hadn't made his will.
He said: 'Nobody warned me to prepare.
You interrupt me, Death; it isn't fair.
You'll have to wait a little. I have still
a grandson's son to make provision for.
My wife would be unhappy if I died

unless she could come with me at my side.
Let me extend my house by one more floor.
Dread lord, you are too hasty.' Death replied:
'Old man, that I surprised you is untrue,
and you were wrong when you complained
of my impatience. Have you not attained
a hundred years of age? Apart from you,
just two perhaps in Paris are as old;
you couldn't find another ten in France.

    You ought, you say, to have been told,
and warned to make arrangements in advance;
I would have found your will already made,
    the money for the grandson paid,
    the building of your mansion finished.
And was it not a warning when in you
the strength to move and walk was much diminished,
    your spirits and your senses too?
They all decline. You cannot taste or hear;
the objects round you fade and disappear.
The daytime star brings light you cannot use,
    the pleasures that you fear to lose
no longer touch you. You have had to see
your friends in illness, near to death, and dead;
what else, do you suppose, might all that be
except a warning? Now then, come with me,
old man; there's nothing further to be said.
    Whether you make your will or not,
    the nation doesn't care a jot.'

I think that Death was right. I would prefer
so old a man, his preparations made,
for seldom can his journey be delayed,
to leave this life behind as if it were
    a banquet where he was a guest,
thanking his host.—Old man, you still protest?
    Then go and watch the young men die.
    They march, they ride, they hurry by

towards their deaths, which it is true
are glorious and brave, but certain too,
and often cruel. But I waste my breath;
you will not hear, however much I strive;
for those who are the least alive
resist the most when facing death.

BOOK VIII.I

THE COBBLER AND THE FINANCIER

A shoemaker sang, through the day, through the year,
a marvel to see and a marvel to hear.
He warbled, he trilled, and he warbled again,
a man more content than all Seven Wise Men.*
Next door, where hoards of gold were kept,
the owner seldom sang; he scarcely slept.
He was a man of finance. In the night
he sometimes would doze off towards first light.
He didn't sleep for long:
the cobbler woke him with a song.
The banker thought it was unfair,
since Providence had taken care
to see that shops have food and drink to sell,
that sleep was not for sale as well.
He told the shoemaker to call,
and asked him: 'Now, good fellow, can you tell
how much, each year, your earnings are in all?'
With a chuckle the jovial shoemaker said:
'My goodness, Your Honour, it isn't my way
to be counting and reckoning day after day,
and if in the end, since each day brings its bread,
I get through the year, that's sufficient for me.'
'Your earnings, then, each day—what might they be?'

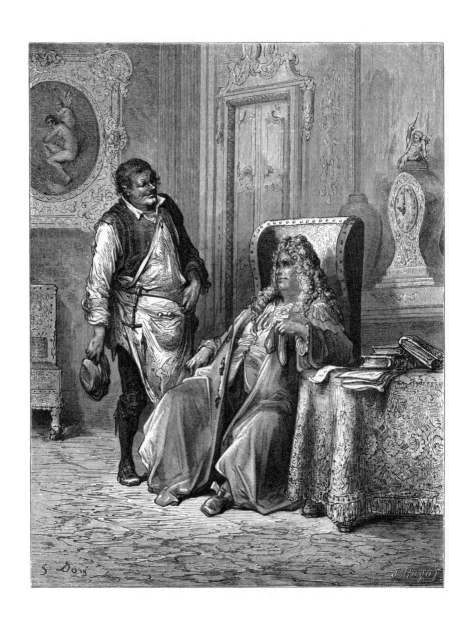

THE COBBLER AND THE FINANCIER

'Now more and now less, on the days I can use.
The trouble is saints' days,* so often they come—
without them I'd earn a respectable sum.
A worshipping day is a day that I lose;
your saints' days are bad for the mending of shoes,
and ever so often when Sunday comes round
the sermon our curé has chosen to preach
   is about a new saint that he's found.'
   On hearing such a candid speech
the banker laughed, and said: 'I want today
   to free you from these ups and downs;
   here are a hundred silver crowns.
   They are for you. Take them away
   to somewhere safe; keep careful guard;
   they'll be of use when times are hard.'
The cobbler thought the earth could not produce,
in centuries, for everybody's use,
   as many silver coins as those.
Back home and to his cellar down he went
to hide his coins, and also his content.
   His voice is lost, his singing goes
     as soon as he obtains
the thing that causes us so many pains.
Sleep leaves his house, which now he shares
with false alarms, suspicion, doubts, and cares.
All day he stays on watch, and if at night
a cat has made a noise, however slight,
the cat is stealing silver from his store.
   At last, so wretched was his plight,
he went to see again the man next door,
whom now his songs awoke no more.
He said: 'I'll give you back these coins to keep,
if you give back my singing and my sleep.'

BOOK VIII.2

THE POWER OF FABLES

To Monsieur de Barillon *

Can an ambassador descend
to reading common tales? Will I offend
by giving you my verse, whose grace relies
on lightness? If at times my poems rise
to grander subjects, will I then be told
    that you consider them too bold?
    The many problems that you face
are distant from the issues in the case
of Rabbit versus Weasel;* read my tale,
    or let it lie; but do not fail
to keep the states of Europe off our hands.
That enemies attack from many lands
    is bound to happen, I agree;
    but that the English wish to see
the friendship that unites our monarchs cease—
    that's something that I can't digest.
Is it not time that Louis had some peace?
What other Hercules would not need rest
from battles with a hydra which can grow
    another head against his every blow?*
    If all your eloquence and tact,
    your subtle thought and skilled advice,
can soften hostile hearts and counteract
this latest threat, then I will sacrifice
a hundred sheep for you: a large amount
for one who lives upon Parnassus' mount.
Meanwhile, to favour me, do not decline
this little incense burnt before your shrine,
    nor turn away if I express
    my ardent hopes for your success,
and offer you this verse, a tale of mine.
    I dedicate it here to you

because the subject seems to fit.
I say no more; the praise that is your due,
   as even Envy must admit,
   you would prefer me to omit.

In Athens once, the people being there
improvident and easy to distract,
a politician rushed to speak, in fear:
he trembled lest the city be attacked.
Desiring in this democratic state
to master the assembly's heart,
he seeks with rhetoric's despotic art
   to force them to confront their fate;
and no one listens. Now he has to choose
   some stronger form of speech to use,
   such as can move the dullest head:
he roars and thunders and invokes the dead,
   says everything that can be said,
     and nobody is stirred:
   the wind makes off with every word.
   The giddy many-headed beast,
   familiar with the tricks it heard,
   was not attending in the least.
   He saw them glancing left and right,
while some were watching children in a fight,
none watching him. To make a fresh appeal
   the speaker chose another way.
   'Our goddess Ceres,'* he began,
'together with a swallow and an eel,
   was on her travels when one day
   they came to where a river ran,
   and had to reach the other side.
   The eel could swim; the swallow flew.'
   As one, the whole assembly cried:
   'And Ceres?—what did Ceres do?'
   'Ceres?' he answered; 'she became
   extremely cross with all of you.

Do you, her people, to your shame,
   care only for a children's tale?
In Philip's war, will only Athens fail,
in all of Greece, to see the risks we run?*
   Why don't you ask what he has done?'
   The fable made the crowd attend,
   and chastened by his reprimand
soon they were at the orator's command;
the tale succeeded for him in the end.
   We're all Athenians at times,
and even as I moralize in rhymes,
if now the tale of Donkey-Skin* were told
I'd stop, and be delighted and beguiled.
They say, and I believe, the world is old;
it still must be diverted like a child.

BOOK VIII.4

WOMEN AND SECRETS

Secrets are heavy, and, for women, are
   too great a load to carry far;
there are some men I know, and not a few,
   who on this point are women too.

To test his wife, a husband loudly cried,
at dead of night, while lying at her side:
'It hurts! the pain is dreadful! What on earth
is happening? Ye gods! I've given birth:
it is an egg.'—'An egg?'—'Yes, yes; look here:
it's fresh; new-laid. Say nothing, though, I pray;
   you've got to keep it secret; swear:
   for otherwise they're bound to say
that I'm a hen. Tell nobody.' The wife,

for whom this strange event was new
(like many other things), believed it true,
and swore herself to silence, on her life.
The promise faded with the shades of night;
for being neither prudent nor discreet,
she rose from bed before the morning light,
and went to find her friend along the street.
'The strangest thing has happened—but,' she said,
'tell nobody: he'll beat me else. In bed,
    last night, my husband laid an egg—
    a big one: twice the usual size.
    In Heaven's name, don't tell, I beg;
just keep it to yourself.' The friend replies:
'Me tell? You're joking. Now, would I betray
    a confidence? Rely on me;
    I won't tell anyone a word.'
    The eggman's wife goes on her way;
    her friend already burns to be
    the bearer of the news she's heard;
she takes it to a dozen houses more.
The clutch of eggs, she says, had numbered three.
Another wife does better: it was four,
she whispers—which she had no need to do,
to guard a secret everybody knew.
    From mouth to mouth the story passed;
    since Mother Gossip travels fast,
    when day was done the husband's score
    had reached a hundred eggs and more.

BOOK VIII.6

THE BEAR AND THE GARDENER

A mountain bear, an ill-formed half-licked bear,*
    once lived—so fate decreed—alone,

and hidden in a forest of his own,
   a new Bellerophon,* was near
to going mad; for reason seldom thrives
   in those who live sequestered lives.
Talking I much esteem, silence no less,
   but both are harmful in excess.
No other animal had business where
   this bear resided in his lair,
   and even being but a bear
this dreary life had brought him to despair.
While melancholy filled this wretched beast,
not far away a man advanced in years
was prey to moods as gloomy as the bear's.
A garden-lover, he was Flora's priest,
and worshipped also at Pomona's shrine*—
good work to do, but which I would combine
with comradeship, some kind and thoughtful friend.
No gardens talk, except in books of mine,
and so the man grew weary, in the end,
of life with beings who remained quite mute,
   and one fine morning, in pursuit
   of somebody who might provide
   some conversation, out he went.
Meanwhile the bear, with similar intent,
had left just then his mountainside.
Around a corner, coming face to face,
   by strange coincidence they met.
The man was scared; without a hiding-place,
what should he do? It was an awkward case:
some Gascon swagger* seemed the safest bet.
He managed therefore to conceal his fear.
The bear, who lacked the social graces, said:
'Come visit, man.' The man replied: 'Lord Bear,
my house is not far distant; should you care
to honour it and visit me instead,
   my rustic meals are yours to share.
Some fruit I have, and milk; it's not the fare

of high-born bears; but what I have, I give.'
The bear accepts. Becoming on the way
good friends at once, they settle in to live
contentedly together; though I'd say
    that it is better, as a rule,
    to live alone than with a fool.
The bear would hardly speak a word all day;
the gardener could work in peace and quiet.
His friend went hunting, varying their diet
with game he brought back home; but what
    he mainly liked to do was swat.
For when the old man rested, he would try
    to keep the space around him clear,
swatting that pest on wings we call a fly.
One day, the gardener was in a doze,
when one such insect much enraged the bear
    by landing on the old man's nose.
Whatever he could do, the fly would stay.
    'I'll get you,' he exclaims, 'this way',
    and then picks up a heavy stone,
    which in the twinkling of an eye,
    adroitly aimed and firmly thrown,
cracking the man's head open, kills the fly.
    As weak in mind as strong in arm,
the bear has stretched him dead upon the ground.
It's dangerous with foolish friends around;
a clever enemy would do less harm.

BOOK VIII.10

THE FUNERAL OF THE LIONESS

King Lion's consort died; and everyone
    came promptly at a run,

respectfully, in order to express
those formal sentiments of consolation
which only bring additional distress.
The lion's messengers, sent far and wide,
announced a funeral commemoration.
      The time and place were specified;
      his officers would be on hand
      to organize the great event,
and tell the mourners where to stand.
I need not tell you: everybody went.
The lion, yielding to his sorrow, roared;
the sound rang round his church, that is, his lair—
lions who own a real church are rare.
      About the court each grieving lord
      in imitation howled or whined,
      each in the jargon of his kind.
      I would define the court a place
in which the residents possess a face
for grief, for laughter, or for anything,
indifferently, to please the king,
becoming what he wishes them to be,
      or if they can't, at any rate
      they show him what he wants to see.
Chameleon-like, like apes, they imitate
their master: here you see control
of many bodies by a single soul,
here men indeed are mere machines.*
But to resume: the stag shed not a tear;
he wasn't sorry, not by any means.
For him, this death was vengeance, since, last year
      his wife and son had been
      the victims of the queen.
      No weeping from the stag, in short.
      One of the sycophants at court
informed on him: he'd seen him laugh, he said.
      A king in anger causes dread,
so Solomon affirms,* and even more

when speaking with a lion's roar;
    but still, the stag was not well-read.
'You woodland vermin,' said the king, 'alone
you laugh, amidst these voices making moan.
    To touch your carcase would demean
our hallowed claw; come, wolves: I call on you
    to take the vengeance that is due,
and sacrifice this traitor to the queen.'
The stag responded: 'Sire, the time to grieve
is over now; your tears, you must believe,
superfluous. A vision have I seen:
I recognized at once, it was so clear,
your gracious consort, lying down, near here,
bedecked in flowers. "Friend," I heard her say,
"you must not let my funeral today
force grief upon you: with the gods I live,
and all the joys Elysium can give
are mine; all creatures here, like me, are blessed.
It pleases me to see the king distressed:
let him still grieve a while."' At this report,
    immediately, around the court,
they cried: 'A miracle!' with one accord;
'the queen's apotheosis is revealed!'
The stag, his sentence now repealed,
    was even given a reward.

    Divert a king with dreams; devise,
        to flatter him, delightful lies;
    you'll bring his fit of anger to an end;
        he'll take the bait; you'll be his friend.

BOOK VIII.14

THE RAT AND THE ELEPHANT

THE RAT AND THE ELEPHANT

Among the French, large numbers are inclined
to think themselves important; many act
like men of consequence; they are in fact
no more than persons of the bourgeois kind.
To silly vanity, we are extremely prone:
it truly is the French disease,* our very own.
Spaniards are vain, but in another way;
their pride, although less foolish, seems in short
   to be the wild fantastic sort.
Our kind is what my characters portray;
it's worth no less than other kinds, I'd say.

A very little rat once chanced to see
an elephant as large as large could be.
He watched the animal of high estate
and mocked its slow and solemn gait.
Upon the triple-tiered creature rode
   a maharanee of renown
on pilgrimage towards a holy town.
   Her household added to the load:
   her dog, her cat, her cockatoo,
   her lady's maid, her monkey too.
   The rat professed to feel surprise
that people should admire this massive hulk.
'As if', he said, 'importance should arise
from filling up more space with greater bulk.
Why are you humans awed to see this sight?
Because its size gives children such a fright?
But in us rats, the fact of being small
does not reduce our self-esteem at all.'
He hadn't finished, but the cat, up high,
   had left her cage and down she came;
   she taught him in an instant why

it isn't sensible to claim
that rats and elephants are just the same.

BOOK VIII.15

THE DONKEY AND THE DOG

Assist each other: Nature rules it so;
but from this rule a donkey once departed.
 The reason why I do not know,
for usually the creature is kind-hearted.
This one, while travelling through country ways,
 in manner solemn, blank of mind,
was with a dog. Their master was behind.
The master went to sleep; the beast to graze.
The grasses in the meadow where they were
 were those that donkeys much prefer.
No thistles, though; for once he did without.
It's not a dish to make a fuss about;
 at banquets, if it should be missed,
 not often do the guests desist.
This time, in short, the grass sufficed for Ned.
Meanwhile the dog was ravenous, and said:
'Dear comrade, for a moment, could you kneel?
The basket that you carry has some bread:
if I could reach it, I could have a meal.'
No answer from the donkey; not a word;
 he made pretend he hadn't heard.
He was, in his Arcadia, afraid
 that if he granted this request
 a bite or two would be delayed.
At last he said: 'My friend, it would be best
to wait; your master, when he wakes from rest,
will see you get your usual food to eat.

He won't be long.' This speech had scarcely ceased
than from the trees appeared another beast:
a wolf, and also much in need of meat.
    He turns at once in their direction.
The donkey asks the dog for his protection.
The dog sits still, and says: 'I would suggest,
my friend, that while your master has his rest
you run away; he won't be very long,
    I'm sure. Take to your heels; be quick.
    And if the wolf should catch you, kick,
and break his jaw. Your hooves, unless I'm wrong,
    are newly shod; you'll knock him flat.'
The donkey, while this speech was being made,
was strangled by the wolf, and that was that.
My moral: come to one another's aid.

BOOK VIII.17

JUPITER AND THE THUNDERBOLTS

Viewing human crime one day
Jupiter was moved to say:
'Other beings must replace,
everywhere that men reside,
this demanding, tiresome race,
plaguing me on every side.
Mercury, you must now go
down to Hades; there below
dwell the Furies; from their den
bring the fiercest. Race of men,
humans I have held too dear,
perish: you will disappear.'
Soon he let his wrath abate.
Kings, whom Jupiter has made

arbiters of human fate,
let your anger be delayed:
let the storm it will create
till next morning comes, be stayed.
Mercury whose wings are light,
Mercury the sweet of voice,
sought the sisters of the night;*
not Tisiphone his choice,
nor Megaera, but the third,
pitiless Alecto. She,
proud to be the one preferred,
swore by Pluto men would be
down within the dark domain
where the gods infernal reign.
Jupiter did not agree.
He dismissed her, but took aim
with a thunderbolt or two
at a certain people who,
lacking faith, had earned his blame.
Since it was their father's hand
aiming lightnings at their land,
they escaped with just a fright:
just one place was set alight,
uninhabited and wild.
Fathers always aim to miss.
What resulted?—only this:
humans, finding Jove so mild,
took advantage and remained
as they were, with no reforms.
All the other gods complained.
He who masses cloud on cloud
promised by the Styx* more storms:
these would never fail, he vowed.
This brought laughter from the rest.
'Father that you are, it's best',
all the gods affirmed, 'to ask
one among us if he'll make

other thunderbolts to shake.'
Vulcan undertook the task.
From his furnaces he brought
thunderbolts diversely wrought.
Some, which never lose their way,
are by gods together hurled
from the sky towards our world.
Others, though, can go astray,
often even getting lost;
only mountains bear the cost;
these ones are the missiles thrown
by the hand of Jove alone.

BOOK VIII.20

THE WOLF AND THE HUNTSMAN

Desire for more, obsession, you whose monstrous eyes
diminish heaven's benefits to pinpoint size,
must I forever fight you vainly in these pages?
Will all my lessons be advice that you avoid?
Will Man, deaf to my voice, as to the Grecian sages,
never declare: 'Enough; for life must be enjoyed'?
    Our lives are short, my friend, do not delay.
    Two words, worth many books, I say again:
    Enjoy yourself.—'Why yes, I will.'—But when?
    'Tomorrow.'—Think, my friend: along the way
    you may meet Death. Enjoy yourself today.
    Take warning from the tale I now relate:
    the Huntsman and the Wolf; beware their fate.

A hunter with his crossbow shot a deer.
A fawn came past, instantly to fall,
and join in death the corpse already there.

THE WOLF AND THE HUNTSMAN

A buck and fawn would make a decent haul,
for one of modest aims it would suffice.
This huntsman sees a splendid wild boar:
another tempting morsel for his store.
At once his latest victim pays the price:
he is despatched towards the Stygian shore,
and yet he still resists the scissor-blade
with which the goddess of the realms below
cuts through our line of life. The Fate delayed
the lethal moment more than once, although
the crossbow's bolt had brought the monster low.

   The hunter now is well supplied,
     but what has ever satisfied
the mighty conqueror's desire for more?
As consciousness awakens in the boar,
across a field a partridge picks her way:
compared to former booty, meagre prey.
The huntsman winds his crossbow just the same,
   and as the boar revives, takes aim.
The tusker now has strength for one last run;
   he charges, rips the man apart,
and dies upon the corpse, his vengeance done.
The grateful partridge thanked him from her heart.

From these mishaps the covetous may learn;
in what comes next the miser has his turn.
A passing wolf observed the piteous sight,
and said: 'I thank you, goddess of good luck!
I'll raise a temple to you on this site.
Four corpses here! What riches have I struck!
But I must husband them for future use:
   such fortunate events are rare.'
For misers this is always their excuse.
   'A good month's eating, I declare,'
the wolf went on, 'this lot provides: one boar,
one buck, one fawn, one human; that makes four,
if I have counted right; a month of meat.

I'll wait two days, and in the meantime eat
the cord upon the crossbow; from the smell
   it must be real catgut, I can tell:
   it's unmistakable.' Which said,
he bit the cord. The crossbow bolt, released,
made one more corpse upon the heap of dead:
it went straight through the bowels of the beast.

My text again: that life should be enjoyed.
Two diverse gluttons jointly were destroyed;
one perished seeking more than he could need,
   the other died from simple greed.

BOOK VIII.27

THE UNFAITHFUL GUARDIAN

By Memory's nine daughters* taught,
I made the animals my theme;
some other heroes might have brought,
perhaps, less honour and esteem.
The wolf and dog, when in my verse,
in language used by gods* converse.
My creatures have their roles to play,
and act for us as best they may.
Some foolish ones there are, some wise,
but those who come in Folly's guise
outnumber others on my page:
her store contains such large supplies.
I also put upon the stage
ungrateful rascals, knaves deceiving,
tyrant bullies, scoundrels thieving,
imprudent boobies by the score,
and flatterers and dupes galore.

The liars I could add as well,
in numbers more than I can tell.
'All men', wrote Solomon the Wise,*
'are liars'; if this fault applies
only in men of low degree,
then at a pinch one might agree;
but that we men are liars all,
without exception, great and small—
were that some other writer's view,
it's one, I think, that I'd deny.
If someone can create a lie
as Aesop and as Homer do,
to call it lying is not right;
these two with wondrous art devise
long dreams to charm and bring delight,
disclosing truth in fiction's guise.
Their books are worthy, I would say,
to last for ever and a day;
if possible, for longer still.
You cannot lie like them at will.
To lie, however, as did once
a trusted agent, whose deceit
resulted in his own defeat,
reveals a villain and a dunce.

It happened thus. A Persian bought and sold.
He went away upon some trade affair,
and left some iron in a neighbour's care.
It was about a hundredweight all told.
Returning home, he asked: 'My iron, then?'
'Your iron? Pardon me; I must admit
it's gone; a rat has eaten every bit.
What could I do? I scolded all my men,
but every barn has holes where rats get through.'
While showing great surprise, the man of trade
pretends to think this miracle is true.
And after waiting for a day or two,

he has the faithless neighbour's son waylaid.
He hides him, then he asks the man to dine.
The father, weeping, says: 'I must decline;
I pray, excuse me; pleasures have I none.
More than my life I loved a boy of mine.
He is my only child.—What did I say?
Alas! no longer do I have a son;
he has been stolen. Pity my despair.'
　　The merchant answered: 'Yesterday,
at dusk, a screech-owl bore your son away.
Towards an ancient building, through the air,
I saw him carried off.' The man replied:
'My son was taken by an owl as prey?
It cannot be. What proof can you provide?
The boy, if need be, could have caught the bird.'
The merchant said: 'The proof of what occurred
I will not give you now. I saw it, though:
I saw it happen, with my very eyes;
　　and seeing that I've told you so
　　no doubt can possibly arise.
If hereabouts there is a rat that ate
a hundredweight of iron, tell me why
it is surprising that an owl can fly
while carrying a boy of half that weight?'
The neighbour saw just what this fiction meant.
Back to the merchant's house the iron went;
back to the neighbour's house his son was sent.

Likewise, two travellers once disagreed.
In telling stories, one was of that class
that seems to use a magnifying-glass:
the things they see are very large indeed.
To hear them, Europe's countries swarm
with beasts like Africa's, of monstrous form.
　　This traveller, in every tale,
preferred to let hyperbole prevail.
　　'I saw a cabbage grow as high',

he told the other, 'as a house.' 'And I',
    replied the second, 'saw a pot
    that's bigger than a church.' 'What rot!'
the first one, jeering, answered. 'No, it's not,'
    the other said; 'it must have been
    to cook the cabbage that you've seen.'

The merchant showed great skill; the other one,
    the pot man, simply had some fun.
    The lesson's this: that when you've heard
    a statement palpably absurd,
    don't try to prove it incorrect,
    for that implies too much respect;
    it's quicker, showing no ill-will,
    to tell a story stranger still.

BOOK IX.I

THE TWO DOVES

Two doves, most fondly loving, lived at home,
till finding it a boring place to be
one took a mad resolve to roam,
and visit distant lands. 'But what of me?'
the other said; 'are we to live apart?
Of all our sorrows, absence is the worst—
    but not for you; you have no heart.
    At least, reflect a little first;
    think of the problems you will find,
the dangers too; perhaps you'll change your mind.
    The year is young, the season cold;
    why all this hurry? Why not wait
for softer winds? Just now the crow foretold
that some poor bird would meet a horrid fate.

Each moment I shall think: what dreadful threat
faces him now? A diving hawk, a trapper's net?
Or if it rains, I'll say: above his head
   is there a roof? Is he well fed?'
The reckless one, affected by this plea,
wavered in his resolve; but in the end
his restless temper and the urge to see
decided him. He said: 'My love, my friend,
no tears; three days at most will satisfy
my spirit's needs, and bring me home again;
we'll soon be reunited, you and I.
I'll tell you my adventures one by one;
we'll have some entertainment then!
   And after all, were I to stay,
what would we have to talk of? We'll have fun
when I describe my travels; I shall say:
"That was a place I saw; what happened here
was this." You'll think that you yourself were there.'
   Then tenderly they said goodbye.
The traveller flew up into the sky;
and as he goes, dark clouds appear.
He must have shelter; none is near,
save one poor tree. Its foliage is thin,
the storm breaks through and soaks him to the skin.
The weather clears enough for him to fly,
and stiff with cold, his feathers drenched by rain,
he does the best he can to get them dry.
   And then he notices some grain,
left scattered in a corner of a field.
   Another dove is standing near.
He lands, attracted by the food that's there,
and he is caught. Some netting was concealed
beneath the treacherous and lying corn.
But since the cords were thin and worn,
   our dove, with beak, with claws, with wing,
   managed at last to break the string.
   Some of his feathers perished too.

Above was worse, for there a vulture flew
with cruel talons ready. He could see
the wretched dove below him, not yet free
from all the trapper's cords; with their remains
dragging around his feet, he looked just like
a prisoner escaping, still in chains.
    The vulture was about to strike,
        when in its turn, from overhead,
an eagle plunged with wings outspread.
Good fortune for the dove: he took to flight,
        and left the brigands to their fight.
He rested by a hovel, feeling glad
    that after what had happened last
    his misadventures should have passed.
    Not so: a rascal of a lad
    (in boyhood pity is unknown)
took up his sling and hit him with a stone.
The dove was only just alive; he cursed
the curiosity he'd felt at first.
    One wing askew, one leg the same,
    he went back home, half-dead, and lame,
    as best he could, and safely came
to home at last, for nothing else occurred
to bring more trouble to the hapless bird.
    With what delights, when reunited,
    the couple's woes were then requited,
    we may well guess, but will not pry.

Oh lovers, happy lovers, and if you
must travel also, go to shores nearby;
be each to each a world forever new,
    forever varied and forever fair.
    No other thing requires your care;
in one another be your all contained.
I too have loved; and then, could I have gained
the Louvre and all the treasures there displayed,
I would have stayed instead in any place,

if only in some woodland glade,
where she had walked or which had seen her face,
     that young and lovely shepherd maid
to whom my promise, never made before,
     enrolled me to the duties done
     by followers of Venus' son.*

Alas! and will such moments come no more?
Oh gentle beings whom I might adore,
     sweet presences, why do I live
a life unsettled by my anxious mind?
Did I but dare to take what love can give!
     Is there no beauty I can find
     to charm my heart and hold it fast?
          Is love for me now past?

BOOK IX.2

THE ACORN AND THE PUMPKIN

Whatever God may do, he does it well.
For proof, no need to search the world all through:
I'll show you in a tale I have to tell
about a pumpkin and a bumpkin, who,
reflecting on this vegetable, thought:
     how huge the fruit, how small the stem!
Said he: 'The Being who created them,
     he didn't do it as he ought;
     that pumpkin's where it shouldn't be.
That fruit, if its creator had been me,
would grow upon an oak, to match its size,
like this oak here. The fruit should suit the tree.
     Our priest says God is very wise;
     a shame he didn't ask me to advise

before he started. Take those acorns now:
he could do better; I'd have shown him how.
They're smaller than my thumb-nail: they belong
upon a little plant, and God was wrong.
    The more I think, the less I doubt
these fruits should be the other way about.'
These thoughts had puzzled John. 'This thinking deep,'
he said, 'it keeps a fellow from his sleep.'
    He settled down beneath the oak,
    and slipped into a gentle doze.
    An acorn fell: it hit his nose,
    and made it hurt; the sleeper woke.
    He groped around his face to see
    how bad the injury might be,
    and found the acorn, which appeared
    to have been caught among his beard.
    Feeling the bruise, he could not choose
    but think again and change his views.
    He cried: 'It scratched me!—just suppose
a heavy weight had fallen on my nose,
a pumpkin, not an acorn, say!—God's laws
prevented it. So he's right: I see the cause
why on a tree a pumpkin never grows.'
And John went homewards, giving praise
    to God on high and all his ways.

BOOK IX.4

THE METAMORPHOSIS OF THE MOUSE

An owl once dropped a mouse while flying by.
Would you have picked her up? No, nor would I;
a Brahmin did, though, which I understand:
ideas will differ in a different land.

This mouse was injured in her fall.
Such fellow-creatures, mice and others,
   concern us little, if at all,
but Brahmins will behave to them like brothers.
This is the doctrine that they have in mind:
a monarch's soul, for instance, taking flight,
may go to animate a tiny mite,
or any creature of some other kind,
as fate may please. This item in their creed
Pythagoras* acquired from them and taught.
   Believing so, the Brahmin thought
   a sorcerer should intercede;
was there a means by which he might restore
the mouse to what she had been once before?
The wizard formed a maiden of fifteen,
   possessed of beauty seldom seen;
lovely enough for Priam's son to take,
   to win himself so fair a prize,
more risks than for the Grecian beauty's sake.*
The Brahmin saw this marvel with surprise,
and to the captivating girl he said:
'You only have to choose whom you will wed,
for any would be honoured and rejoice
   were we to offer him your hand.'
She answered him: 'If that is how things stand,
the one with greatest power is my choice.'
The Brahmin knelt before the sun and cried:
'Oh sun, my daughter is to be your bride.'
'Not so: that darkening cloud can hide my face;
he is more powerful,' replied the sun;
'I recommend you take him in my place.'
The Brahmin called upon the cloud on high:
'Well then, are you by destiny the one
to wed this girl?' 'Alas!' he said, 'not I:
   the wind obliges me to fly
just as he wishes, over hill and dale;
   the rights of Boreas* prevail.'

The Brahmin, vexed, cried out: 'If that's the case,
   you wind, come quickly while you may,
     to take this girl in your embrace.'
The wind bore down: a mountain blocked his way.
In turn the mountain kept the ball in play.
'If I accept,' he said, 'I'd give offence,
and irritate the rat, which makes no sense,
   seeing that he can pierce my side.'
The girl took notice, hearing of a rat;
   she chose him and became his bride.
—A rat?—A rat: for that's what love can do;
for instance Lady This or Madam That:*
but keep it quiet; that's just between us two.
Your origins will surely be revealed:
for that idea, the tale gives strong support;
but when you look at it, you find a sort
   of sophistry, not quite concealed.
For if you argue in this fable's way,
then any husband has a better right
   than did the sun. Am I to say
a giant has less power than a flea
because the flea can live on him and bite?
Had he behaved with justice, Master Rat
   would not have claimed the bride-to-be:
he should have passed her to the stronger cat;
then onward to the hound she'd go; from hound
to wolf. The tale would keep on going round;
   we'd finish where we had begun:
the maiden would be taken by the sun.
Now for metempsychosis: in my view
what happened when the wizard cast his spell
does not support the Brahmin's doctrine well,
   but shows it rather false than true.
For on his principles, so I would claim,
the souls of men, of mice, of worms, perforce
   are taken from a common source,
their origins supposedly the same;

but yet, inserted in each creature's frame,
　　what differences confront our eyes!
　　While some go crawling, others rise.
The maiden's soul, residing in such beauty,
　　should surely have performed its duty,
and properly she should have wed the sun;
it was the rat, we're told, that took her heart.
But rodent souls, when all is said and done,
are from the souls of maidens far apart.

Our destiny defines us, every one—
by which I mean the laws that Heaven made.
　　Consult the Devil, ask his aid,
cast magic spells; they do not have the force
to turn a creature from its natural course.

BOOK IX.7

THE OYSTER AND ITS CLAIMANTS

One day two pilgrims saw upon the sand
an oyster that the tide had brought to land.
Their fingers point, their eyes devour the prey;
as for their stomachs, differences arise.
Just as the one bends down to take his prize
　　the other pushes him away.
'We need', he says, 'a rule to make it clear
by whom this oyster is to be enjoyed.
The one who first perceived it lying there
will eat; the other watches.'—'In that case,
　　if that's the rule to be employed,'
　　his comrade says, 'I thank God's grace
that I possess good eyes.'—'I as well,'
the other one replies, 'and I can tell
　　I saw it first; to that I'd swear.'

THE OYSTER AND ITS CLAIMANTS

'All right: you may have seen it; but by smell
   I recognized it in advance.'
While thus in keen debate they persevere,
Judge Peter Dandy* comes along by chance.
They ask if he will settle the affair.
He splits the shell; and then with solemn air
he gobbles up the object in dispute.
As grave as Solomon, the meal concluded,
he tells them: 'To each claimant in this suit
the Court gives half the shell. Costs are excluded.
And now the parties may, in peace, withdraw.'

Count what it costs today to go to law;
ask families who suffer this expense
how much remains to them: you'll see
that Dandy keeps the pounds to pay his fee;
   he leaves the litigants the pence.

BOOK IX.9

THE TREASURE AND THE TWO MEN

A man lacked credit and resources; worse,
for cash he had the Devil in his purse,
I mean, he'd nothing left to spend.
To hang himself, he thought, would do some good:
he'd have some choice of how his woes would end,
because, if he did not decide, starvation would;
to die of hunger is of slight attraction,
   except to people who are keen
to taste their death. A ruin was the scene
he chose to put his project into action.
He took with him a nail to fix the noose
high up inside, upon a certain wall.
   This wall was old, its stones were loose.

As soon as it is struck it starts to fall,
and crumbles: treasure that had been inside
falls too. At once our would-be suicide
collects it, leaves the noose, but doesn't stay:
he takes the gold, not bothering to count;
he fancies it whatever the amount.
And while the fellow swiftly went his way,
the treasure's owner entered, whereupon
    he found his riches gone.
'Shall I not die?' he cried, 'my hidden hoard
is lost; shall I not hang? I shall indeed;
   a length of rope is all I need.'
   And there beside him lay the cord;
   the noose was waiting, ready-made;
it only lacked a neck. With his inside
it well and truly hanged him, and he died.
The rope was someone else's, who had paid:
by this, perhaps, the miser was consoled.
The rope had changed its owner, like the gold.

Few misers end their days except in grief.
In what they hoard they have the smallest share;
to others go the fruits of all their care—
to kinsfolk, or the earth, or to a thief.
And what about the neat exchange
that Fortune managed to arrange?
She does enjoy these little tricks of hers;
   and when the consequence is strange
   it's what the lady much prefers.
The fickle goddess thought she'd like to see
a fellow hanging; and the man affected
   must have found his death to be
    completely unexpected.

BOOK IX.16

THE TWO RATS, THE FOX, AND THE EGG

Two rats went looking for some food, and found
    an egg upon the ground;
for people of that kind, sufficient fare;
it's not as if they had to have an ox.
    With appetite, and much delight,
    they each prepared to take his share,
when who should come in view but Mister Fox.
    Unlucky chance! unwelcome sight!
    How could they guard their egg intact?
If both stood upright, might it then be packed
in wrapping of some kind that they could hold,
    with paws stretched out, between each other,
and walk with it? Could it be dragged? Or rolled?
Impossible, it seemed, and risky too.
Necessity, invention's clever mother,
    resolved the problem what to do.
The robber being half a mile away,
they still had time to reach their dwelling-place.
One rat lay down, and in a close embrace
he hugged the egg; the other, as he lay,
despite the bumps endangering his back,
then pulled him by his tail along the track.

    I'll stand by what my tale has taught:
mere animals possess the power of thought.

BOOK IX, last (extract from the concluding *Discourse for
Mme de La Sablière*)

THE MAN AND THE SNAKE

A man perceived a snake.
'You brute!' he cried, 'the action I shall take
will be approved throughout the universe.'
   Then of the two the more perverse,
the snake (but if you thought the man was meant,
you were, quite understandably, mistaken),
   the snake, then, let itself be taken.
   Once caught, into a sack it went,
and what was worse, it was condemned to die,
guilty or not; although the man did try
   to prove that right was on his side;
   he uttered this harangue: 'In you
we see ingratitude personified.*
I say it is a foolish thing to do
to treat the wicked well; you die, therefore.
Your spite, your teeth, will injure me no more.'
   In serpent language, from his sack,
as best he could the serpent answered back:
'If none who are ungrateful are to live,
      then whom would we forgive?
This is a lesson that you humans have instilled:
you'll see it if you look. I can be killed
by you, at any time, because the test
of human justice is: what suits you best;
your pleasure; your caprice. By laws like these
I am condemned. At least permit me, please,
to say, in death, as plainly as I can:
the symbol of ingratitude is man,
and not the serpent.' His reflections caused
some hesitation in the other, and he paused,
but said at length: 'Your comments lack foundation.
I have the right to give my verdict now,
but let us take the case to arbitration.'

The snake agreed. Nearby there stood a cow.
They call her over so that they can ask:
which one is right? This was a simple task.
    'Why bother me for that?' she said;
    'it is the snake; why should I lie?
    This man for many years I fed.
    For him no single day went by
without the benefits that I supply;
and all for him. My milk, the calves I bore,
brought him back home with money in his purse;
I helped him when, with age, his health grew worse.
    With all his needs provided for,
my toils ensured that he had pleasures too.
And now he keeps me, as I end my days,
    without a blade of grass to chew.
If only there were somewhere I could graze!—
    but I am tethered to a stake.
    Suppose my master were a snake:
would his ingratitude have gone as far?
Farewell; you asked my views; and there they are.'
Amazed to hear her judgment, and aggrieved,
the man exclaimed: 'Old fool! she's off her head.
    Why should such dotards be believed?
Let's ask this ox.'—'Agreed,' the serpent said.
No sooner said than done. The ox approached
    slowly; and once the case was broached,
he ruminated on it, saying then
that he had laboured long, and had been bound
to burdens shouldered for the good of men;
had ever trod the seasons' course of toil,
    their endless cycle bringing round
    the gifts from Ceres to our soil,
which we have free, while animals must pay.
Then as reward for all the work he'd done,
he'd had few thanks, but beatings every day,
from every man he'd seen, bar none,
    and now that he was old, they thought

he should feel honoured when his blood was shed
so that the gods' indulgence might be bought.*
The ox fell silent, and the human said:
'I've had enough of hearing him declaim;
he comes to preach and make some grand effect,
but does not mean to judge: he means to blame.
    His verdict therefore I reject.'
      But when they asked the tree
        to act as referee,
things grew still worse: against the summer's heat,
against the wind and rain when tempests beat,
the tree replied, he sheltered us. His shade
    was not the only gift he made:
    for us alone he beautified
    our gardens and the countryside;
    his boughs hung low with fruit. And yet
    the sole reward that he would get
was that some woodman cut him to the ground.
    Such was his pay, although, year round,
    he freely gave us all his treasures:
the fruits of autumn, blossom in the spring;
in summer, shade; in winter, fireside pleasures.
    Why not, instead of felling, bring
    the pruning-saw? He was robust; if pruned,
    he'd soon recover from the wound.
Annoyed, his argument appearing lost,
the man resolved to win at any cost.
'I am too kind; I was a fool', he said,
    'to let these creatures talk at all.'
    He hit the sack against a wall
    until the snake inside was dead.

Thus do the great behave. Fixed in their heads
is this belief: that men and quadrupeds,
    and serpents like the rest,
are born for them. If any dare protest,
they're being foolish.—I agree; they are.—

What course of action, then, do you suggest?—
Speak not a word, or speak it from afar.

BOOK X.1

THE TORTOISE AND THE TWO DUCKS

A tortoise, frivolous of mind,
resolved to travel; home she found a bore.
Often do foreign lands attract us more;
often at home do cripples feel confined.
She told two ducks about her novel plan.
'We'll help you, ma'am,' they answered, 'if we can.
Observe, above, our spacious thoroughfare:
we'll fly you to America as freight.
    You'll see below you, from the air,
    many a country, many a state.
From viewing people's varied customs too
    you'll find that many benefits accrue.
    Great Ulysses once did the same.'
It isn't often that one hears the name
of Ulysses referred to by a duck.
The parties all agree; a deal is struck.
As for the method that the ducks devise
    to loft their tourist through the skies,
they find a stick on which she is to bite
when placed between her teeth. 'Just hold on tight,'
    they say, 'and mind you don't let go.'
The ducks then grasp the stick's projecting ends,
and up they fly; the tortoise too ascends.
    This scene brought much surprise below:
the people saw the creeping creature fly,
complete with house, the ducks on either side.

'A miracle! Just look up there!' they cried;
   'the queen of tortoises is in the sky!'
'The queen? It's true! I am the tortoise queen;
and treat me with respect.' She would have been
   more sensible to hold her peace.
   For since she had unclenched her teeth
   this action forced her to release
   the stick she held, and down she fell,
   towards the watching crowds beneath,
   and in her fall destroyed her shell.
   Imprudence causing her demise,
   she met her death before their eyes.
Thus empty curiosity is tied
to boastful chatter, carelessness, and pride;
all from one stock, related creatures,
like children who inherit family features.

BOOK X.2

THE FISHES AND THE CORMORANT

   A cormorant had never failed to take
   from every near or distant lake
   a contribution to his daily fare,
      each pond and pool had paid its share.
      And so this bird could eat his fill;
   but as the number of his years increased
      they froze the creature stiff and still;
      the standard of cuisine decreased.
   Upon themselves do cormorants rely
   in order to maintain their food supply,
   but lacking nets or traps of any kind,
   the fish too deep for aged eyes to find,
   what could he do, with nothing left to eat?

Need is an expert teacher of deceit:
it taught him this. Beside a lake one day
    he saw a crayfish. 'Friend,' he said,
    'please take this message straight away
to all who live down there. They'll soon be dead.
    Next week the owner of this place
will come to fish these waters through.'
    The crayfish goes at once, apace,
to spread the news; he spread much panic too.
    The fishes scurried, met, conferred,
    and delegates were sent. 'Sir Bird,'
    they asked, 'is this report quite true?
By whom were you informed? Can it be proved?
Is there some remedy? What can we do?'
    'You must', the bird replied, 'be moved.'
    'We move? but how can that be done?'
'Don't worry. I will take you, one by one,
to my retreat. Its whereabouts are known
    to God and to myself alone.
    No shelter could be more secure.
This pool carved out by Nature from the stone,
unseen by faithless humans, will ensure
your whole community's salvation.'
The members of the water-dwelling nation
believed what he had told them, every word,
and each in turn was carried by the bird
to waters by a cliff, remote and steep.
The cormorant, their bringer of good news,*
now had them in his private pool, not deep,
but narrow and transparent: he could choose,
each day, which fish to take and which to keep.
From him they learned this lesson, to their cost:
not to entrust yourself to those who treat
    people as something good to eat.
    But for these fish not much was lost:
the human wolf-pack would have taken care
    to gobble plenty for its share.

If someone eats you, does it matter who,
of wolf or man? All bellies, I would say,
    are equal in the victim's view;
if you're devoured tomorrow or today,
there's little difference between the two.

BOOK X.3

THE WOLF AND THE SHEPHERDS

A wolf in whom humanity held sway
    (if such can be, in such a breed)
    reflected deep and long one day
    on all the cruel things he'd done,
    albeit forced on him by need.
'They hate me, all of them,' he said, 'bar none:
wolves are public enemy number one.
In villages men meet with horse and hound
to hunt us down, and Jupiter on high
    is deafened with the hue and cry.
In England not a wolf is to be found:*
by order, killing wolves has earned a fee.
    So local squires, one and all,
    attack us with the same decree,
while mothers threaten, if their children bawl,
    to give them to the wolf for tea.*
    And what is all this fuss about?
Some scabby donkey or some poxy sheep,
some snarling cur. Such morsels they can keep:
not food for me; I'd sooner go without.
So be it then: henceforth I shall abstain
from eating creatures that have life and breath.
I'll browse instead, and live on grass and grain;
or rather, starve and die. Is such a death

so cruel? Better that, at any rate,
   than facing universal hate.'
Some shepherds were nearby, and when he looked,
he saw them eating meat that they had cooked:
they'd grilled some lamb. 'Now, what's all this?' he said;
'I blame myself for all the blood I shed,
while those who have these creatures in their care
devour them? And they give their dogs a share!
Must I then scruple still, wolf that I am,
to take my meat? By all the gods, not so!
I'd look absurd. I'll have that little lamb:
no need to cook him, down my throat he'll go;
so will the mother suckling him, that ewe.
   I'll have the ram his father too.'

This wolf was right: is there a law to say
that we can gorge ourselves on any prey,
take animals for food, while they retreat
back to the Golden Age, forgoing meat?*
No grills or cooking-pots for them, say you?—
shepherds, reflect: the wolf is only wrong
   when he is weak and you are strong.
   Why should he live as hermits do?

BOOK X.5

THE TWO ADVENTURERS AND THE TALISMAN

No paths bedecked with flowers lead to glory.
Think of the tasks that Hercules despatched;*
   this hero's feats are scarcely matched
   in any history, or even story.
I find just one example close to hand:
a travelling adventurer who read

a talismanic script and thus was led
to seek his fortune in a fabled land.
He and a comrade found a standing pole
    bearing a board that bore this scroll:
'You who adventure here need do no more,
    should you desire to see a sight
    unseen by any wandering knight,
than cross this torrent to its further shore.
There lies a sculpted elephant of stone:
lift it and climb the mountain, on your own,
not taking breath, until you reach, on high
its summit, proudly threatening the sky.'
The comrade got cold feet, and said: 'The stream
is no less deep than rapid, it would seem,
and when you've swum across as best you can,
    you get an elephant as prize:
a load of trouble. What a stupid plan!
The elephant must be the shape and size
that you might carry twenty feet or so;
but in one breath, right up the mountain—no:
no mortal man could do so strange a stunt;
unless the model were a dwarf or runt,
a pygmy elephant, the kind you see
carved as the handle for a walking-stick.
If that's your load, where would the glory be?
The message on the scroll must be a trick,
some riddle for a child. And that is why
I'll leave the elephant to you: goodbye.'
    His rational companion gone,
our bold adventurer pays little heed
to warnings of the water's depth and speed,
but plunges in, eyes closed, and presses on;
    the river crossed, he sees ahead
the elephant, just as the scroll had said.
Picking it up, he climbs without a stop,
    and sees, arriving at the top,
a citadel behind a walled parade.

The elephant cries out; and at its call
armed citizens appear along the wall.
The bravest knight might well have fled, dismayed,
   but this one vowed to make a stand,
and die a hero's death with sword in hand.
   He was astonished when he heard
   that now, their monarch being dead,
   they would proclaim him king instead.
   Out of decorum, he demurred;
the task might be, he said, beyond his scope.
Sixtus* declared the same when chosen pope.
   (Can it be such a woeful thing
   to be elected pope or king?)
   His words, as soon became quite clear,
   had been a little insincere.

Blind courage has blind Fortune at his side.
It's sometimes wise to act and take a chance
at once, and not let wisdom be your guide,
nor scrutinize your action in advance.

BOOK X.13

AN ADDRESS TO M. DE LA ROCHEFOUCAULD

I often think, observing how men act,
   and how in almost all respects
   mankind's behaviour reflects
the lower creatures' habits, that in fact
   this king of animals, whom all obey,
   has just as many faults as they.*
Nature has placed, in creatures high and low,
some granules she has taken from the dough
that fashions mind—I mean the body's mind,

AN ADDRESS TO M. DE LA ROCHEFOUCAULD

created out of matter much refined.*
To prove what I have said, let me explain.

When hunters watch, perhaps while daylight's rays
    sink down into the watery main,
or when the sun begins to bring some light
before full day, and while the night still stays,
I climb at forest's edge among the trees,
a modern Jove on this Olympian height,
with thunderbolt in hand, and as I please
strike dead some rabbit, unaware beneath.
At once his tribe abruptly disappears
from where, with eyes alert and pricked-up ears,
they had been playing on the grassy heath
and fragrant thyme had sweetened their repast.
    Sent running by the gunshot blast,
    they go where safety can be found,
    within their fortress underground.
The danger, though, is soon forgotten there,
    and with it they forget their fear:
    I watch as they emerge again;
    more playful than before they frisk
    in front of me, and still at risk.
So are they not identical to men?—
our shipwrecked seamen, scarcely back on shore,
will risk another wreck, another gale;
you see them go aboard and setting sail,
    surrendering themselves once more
to Fortune's hands, just as my rabbits do.
    Or take another common case:
    when dogs are strangers in some place
outside their territory, and passing through,
imagine the festivities that start;
with yelps and snarling jaws the local hounds,
who have their bellies' interests at heart,
will see them off beyond the parish bounds.
So too with men who trade, or govern states,

or serve at court: their interest relates
to money, or to grandeur, or to fame,
but interest determines how they act,*
and in the rest of us you see the same.
The newcomer is threatened and attacked—
which custom both coquettes and writers share.
    Aspiring authors should beware.
    The fewer present round the cake,
the more for each. We play for our own sake:
    that's what the game is all about.

A dozen more examples could attest
    the truth of what I say, no doubt;
but as the masters of my art* have taught
    the shortest works are always best,
and verses on the richest subjects ought
    to leave some further scope for thought.
      Here then this piece will close.
      To you, my lord, it owes
whatever it contains of real weight,
you who, as modest as your rank is great,
find any praise uncomfortable to bear,
however just, well-founded, or sincere;
who only with reluctance would consent
that I should offer homage to you here in rhyme;
whose name defends my works and will prevent
the damage done by critics and by time,
and being known in other lands and days
has brought to France herself its share of praise,
    this country that has given birth
to more great names than any land on earth.
Allow me, then, at least, to make it clear
    that you supplied my subject here.

BOOK X.14

THE LION

Sultan Leopard once possessed,
because, it seems, of many a bequest,
herds of deer in woodland; in the field
as many cattle; sheep across the weald.
One day was born, in forest land near there,
a royal lion cub. The Sultan sent
the usual compliments on this event,
as monarchs should; then spoke with his vizier,
a wise old fox, a practised politician.
'You fear our neighbour, this new cub,' he said,
'but why? What can he do, in his position?
He is an orphan; with his father dead,
we ought, poor child, to pity him instead.
He has at home much trouble on his hands;
so far from conquering another state,
he ought to feel much gratitude to Fate
    if he can simply hold his lands.'
Stroking his chin, the fox said: 'Pity, Sire,
is not what orphans of that kind inspire
in me. We should arrange to be his friend,
or that he meets with an untimely end.
Act now, before he grows his teeth and claws,
    to stop the damage he can cause.
    The matter cannot be delayed,
for from his horoscope, which I have made,
    he will be great through war, I find,
and loyal, more than any of his kind,
    towards his friends. You ought to seek
either to be his friend, or make him weak.'
The warning was in vain. The Sultan, then,
was sleeping; sleeping, too, both beasts and men
    throughout the country; and at length
the cub, full grown, acquired a lion's strength.
Forthwith alarm bells ring on every side;

against him, trumpets sound the call to war.
The fox was summoned to advise. He sighed,
and said: 'These moves inflame the lion more.
They cannot help. It's useless, I'm afraid,
to call up reinforcements to our aid.
The more we get, the more they cost to keep;
they're good for nothing but to eat your sheep.
Appease the lion: on his own, his powers
can vanquish all these mercenaries of ours.
We pay these allies; he requires just three:
his vigour, strength, and courage, which are free.
Pay tribute: drive a sheep between his jaws.
If that does not appease him, do not pause,
but send another. Also send an ox,
and for these gifts, among your herds and flocks
    select the fattest and the best.
    By giving these you save the rest.'
The Sultan did not care for this advice;
    he and the others paid the price.
    In his and every neighbour state
    there were no gains; the loss was great.
This world of enemies did not suffice
to hold the lion back; what could be done
they did; but he who caused their terror won.
Where lions are concerned, if you intend
to let one grow, make sure he is your friend.

BOOK XI.I

THE DREAM OF ONE WHO LIVED IN
MOGUL LANDS

A subject of the Mogul saw in dream
Elysium: and there stood a vizier;
the joys he had were lasting, pure, extreme.

He saw, this dreamer, in another place
a hermit plunged in flame, pain so severe
that others damned felt pity for his case.
The sight was unexpected, seemed absurd;
in sentencing the dead had Minos* erred?
The sleeper woke, so much was he surprised,
but guessing that these scenes contained
  some mystery disguised
 he asked to have the dream explained.
'You need not be perturbed,' the sage replied.
'If what I know of dreams is any guide,
you have received a message, heaven-sent,
on how these two behaved before they died.
For this vizier would frequently resort
to quiet retreat; that hermit* often went
to curry favour with viziers at court.'

To this interpretation dare I add,
 to favour lovers of retreat,
some words about the blessings to be had
in loving it? Untrammelled, pure and sweet,
a gift from Heaven, open at our feet.
Oh solitudes, you offer hidden joys;
places forever loved, when will I gaze,
remote from others and their noise,
 upon your cool, secluded ways?
Who will assist me to behold again
your sheltering shades, and there remain?
When will the Muses be my sole concern,
when shall I, far from court and business, learn
 the diverse movements of the skies,
 their secrets kept from human eyes,
the manner how those shifting lights are named,
the diverse qualities that they possess
by which our customs and our lives are framed?*
 And if such elevated themes
should be beyond my powers, nonetheless

there will be beauty yet along the streams;
let me but see it; let my verses show
some river's edge on which the flowers grow.
The Fates may weave some lives with golden thread,
not mine; the room where I shall lay my head
will not be richly panelled; is my sleep
worth less, or less delicious, or less deep?
 New sacrifices I will make,
  I vow it for seclusion's sake.
When free from care my life has run its course
to meet the dead will bring me no remorse.

  BOOK XI.4

THE DANUBE PEASANT

Do not judge others by the way they look.
 It's good advice, although not new.
Already I have used, to prove it true,
the creatures that my little mouse mistook.
Aesop and Socrates* will serve at present,
with someone else as well, a certain peasant,
who lived beside the Danube. You have heard
about the first two; as regards the third,
Marcus Aurelius, no less, portrayed*
 his looks in detail. I have made
 a shorter version. On his chin
 there grew an ample, spreading beard.
 In general, the man appeared,
 so very hairy was his skin,
 most like a bear, although, in truth,
 a bear misshapen and uncouth.
His glance was, under bushy brows, cross-eyed;
he had a drooping lip; his nose was bent.

Around the goatskin cloak he wore
   a belt of plaited reeds was tied.
This was the envoy that his fellows sent
from where they lived close by the Danube's shore.
What distant towns were not beneath the yoke
of mighty Rome, and Roman greed? He went,
   therefore, to Rome, and thus he spoke:
   'Romans, and you who are arrayed,
oh senators, to hear me: first I pray
to all the gods to offer me their aid;
may the Immortals be my guides today,
and keep me free from blame for what I say.
Without the gods' assistance men resort
to wickedness and vice of every sort;
those who neglect the gods must break their laws.
My nation will bear witness: we indeed
are sorely punished by your Roman greed,
and of our woes our crimes must be the cause,
not Roman feats of arms. Beware, beware,
   oh Romans, lest the gods prepare
a vengeance on you, and, in future years
make Rome experience our grief and tears,
   and in their wrath, by just redress,
   give us the power which in turn
   will make you slaves whom we oppress.
Why we should now be yours I cannot learn;
   are Romans then of greater worth
than all the diverse peoples of the earth?
What right do they possess to be obeyed
across the world? And why should you invade
a life of innocence? In peace we tilled
our happy regions, and our hands were skilled
   in every art, as with the plough.
   What have the Goths learned from you now?
Our courage and adroitness are well known,
   and if like you we had been schooled
in violence and greed, we might have ruled

instead of you, and would have shown
less barbarism than your praetors* do.
Their deeds are hard even to comprehend;
the cruelties that they commit offend
    the very shrines revered by you.
The gods, oh Romans, watch us from the skies,
and only scenes of horror meet their eyes,
because of the examples you have set.
They see their temples and themselves disdained;
they see gross avarice left unrestrained.
Your officers' demands cannot be met;
    we waste our labour and our lands
in vain attempts to fill their grasping hands.
Withdraw these men: we will no longer toil,
on their behalf, for produce from our soil.
Our towns are empty now; our men have fled
towards the hills. They shun their cherished wives
and dwell among the savage beasts instead,
for fear they will create unhappy lives,
and populate a land oppressed by Rome.
    As for our children still at home,
    we hope they die before their time.
Thus do your praetors force us into crime,
besides despair. Withdraw them; what we learn
from them is vice and luxury; in turn
the Goths will be like them, a greedy race.
In Rome I saw the same, around this place,
as soon as I arrived; unless your cause
provides an opportunity for gain,
for gold or honours, you will seek in vain
for justice or protection from the laws,
and justice done will always be delayed.
This speech, oh Senators, that I have made
is blunt, and has begun, so I suspect,
    to give offence. I end it here.
Death is the punishment that I expect
for speaking in a manner too sincere.'

He cast himself before them on the ground;
and all sat dumb, amazed that they had found,
in this rough savage, who before their eyes
lay prostrate now, a mind so wise,
a tongue so eloquent, a man so brave.
Their praetors were replaced. To him they gave
patrician rank*—a vengeance, it was thought,
well suited to the speech that they had heard.
The Senate had it copied, word for word:
a model for their speakers to be taught
in future ages; but, in speaking well,
    the Romans did not long excel.

BOOK XI.7

THE OLD MAN AND THE THREE YOUNGSTERS

A man aged eighty-plus was planting trees.
   'Were he to build,' said three young men
from local families, passing by just then,
'it might make sense; but planting, if you please!
A man his age!—he's senile, that's quite plain.
   Tell us just what you stand to gain
from all your work? Your life would have to last
as long as Abraham's. Why take such care
to shape a future which you cannot share?
   It is your errors of the past
which you should ponder now. Far-reaching schemes
you must give up; give up expansive dreams;
   such projects are for us alone.'
   'For you?' the old man answered; 'no:
whatever riches we may own,
   we get them late; they quickly go.
     The Fates who dwell below

THE OLD MAN AND THE THREE YOUNGSTERS

with pallid hands make sport
of numbering our days, and favour none,
not me, not you; our lives are, every one,
    alike in being soon cut short.
Who will be last among us, you or I,
to see the azure brightness of the sky?
As every moment goes, how do we know
that we shall live when it has passed?
My grandsons and their sons will owe
    to me the shade these trees will cast.
    When men are wise, and toil to give
some pleasant thing to others, will you say
that they should not? This work I do today
gives me enjoyment also. If I live,
it will again tomorrow, and, maybe,
for some time longer still. The morning light
might even shine some few days more for me
across your graves.'—The old man's words proved right.
    One youngster planned to cross the sea
to Canada: he drowned, still close to shore.
Another was ambitious to advance
    towards high offices of state.
He served his country on the field of war,
and taken unawares by evil chance
was shot and killed. The third one met his fate
when having climbed high up a tree
to take a graft, he slipped and missed his hold.
The old man wept, while writing for the three,
        as epitaph, the fable I have told.

BOOK XI.8

ODYSSEUS AND HIS COMPANIONS

To His Highness the Duke of Burgundy *

Although, my lord, your welfare is the care
uniquely of immortals, let me share
   in adding incense to your shrine.
   My age and labours may excuse
the lateness of these presents from my muse;
the passing years have shrunk these wits of mine.
With you, meanwhile, we watch as they advance
faster and faster; almost taking wing.
That hero, he from whom your virtues spring,
would also speed ahead, had he the chance;
he burns to follow Mars upon the field,
and giantlike make adversaries yield,
earn glory, winning victories for France.
Some power holds him back, some force divine:
   our King; who in a month, no more,
   became the master of the Rhine.
Such speed was necessary in that war;
it might seem rash today. In any case,
a lecture on such things is out of place:
the gods of love and laughter, by report,
   prefer discussions to be short;
they are the deities who fill your court.
They never leave your side; although it's clear
that other powers too are worshipped there,
for all is ruled by reason and good sense.
Consult these two regarding some events
when certain Greeks, with little care or thought,
surrendered to temptation, and were caught
   by potent magic charms; they then
metamorphosed, becoming beasts, not men.

Odysseus and his comrades, plagued by fears,
had sailed directionless for ten long years,

blown by the winds. They reached an unknown bay;
and here the daughter of the god of day,
Circe,* held court. Delicious to the taste,
 the drink she offered them was laced:
she'd poisoned it. At once it took away
 their human reason; then, in place
 of bodies with a human face,
 they soon had those of other creatures,
 other shapes and other features.
 What formerly were men appear
 as lion, elephant, or bear,
 some huge like these, or very tall,
and some, the mole for instance, rather small.
 The sorceress transformed them all
but one: only Odysseus stopped to think
that treachery might lurk in Circe's drink.
 Odysseus was not only wise,
 but eloquent; he had the look
 that heroes have, and Circe took
that poison as she gazed into his eyes
which makes its victims, like the one she brewed,
helpless. A goddess dares to speak her mind;
this one spoke love. Odysseus was too shrewd,
in such a situation, not to find
an opportunity to help his men;
he asked, and she consented to restore
the forms and faces they had had before.

'But will they really want them back again?'
the nymph enquired; 'why don't you make quite sure,
and put it to them now?' So straight away
Odysseus hurried to the lion, to say:
'For Circe's poisoned cup there is a cure;
you can decide to be a man once more.
Already you have gained the power to speak.'
The lion spoke, though meaning still to roar:
 'Is my intelligence so weak?

Renounce my new-found strength, my teeth and claws?
My enemies I butcher, piece by piece.
I am the King of Beasts; and for what cause
would I become a subject in your Greece?
—and still a soldier, should you so dictate.
    I have no wish to change my state.'

Odysseus hastened off to see the bear.
'My friend, what has become of you!' he cried;
'and you so handsome once!' The bear replied,
in bearish tones: 'And why have you come here?
Is it to let me know that you object
to my appearance? What do you expect?
    My looks are what a bear's should be.
Why should a certain shape and face
be uglier than others? Why should we
be judged by members of the human race?
Go to a she-bear and enquire from her
which lover, of us two, she would prefer.
    If you dislike my looks, why stay?
    Leave me in peace and go away.
    I have no cares, and no one to obey;
I'm happy and I'm free; I tell you straight
    I have no wish to change my state.'

Despite the risk of one refusal more,
the Grecian prince proceeded to address
the wolf, and put the question as before.
'Comrade,' he said, 'it causes me distress
to listen to a fair young shepherdess
bewailing to the winds the way you feed
upon her sheep, with such rapacious greed.
Before, you would have guarded them instead:
it was an honourable life you led.
    Renounce the woods, and once again
    rejoin the ranks of honest men.'
'Of honest men?' the wolf said; 'I see few

of that description; but I know your view
of wolves: bloodthirsty beasts, you say; and you?
   You would devour, I have no doubt,
   the sheep the village weeps about,
except that I was first. Come now, confess:
were I a man, would I love carnage less?
You men behave like wolves to other men:
you sometimes kill each other for a word.*
   If we're comparing villains, then
   I'll tell you which should be preferred:
a wolf's existence is the better fate.
   I do not wish to change my state.'

   Odysseus said the same to each.
   In turn, without exception, all,
   the larger creatures and the small,
   gave the same answer to his speech.
   To roam the forest unrestrained,
   to satisfy their appetites,
   to them were the supreme delights;
they all refused the honour to be gained
by noble deeds. They thought they had freewill,
but they were captives of their passions still.

To end, my lord, the subject that I sought
   was one that would instruct and please;
   a good idea, or so I thought,
   could I have hit on one with ease.
The comrades of Odysseus came to mind:
this lowly world has many of their kind.
The punishment which is their due
is to be hated and despised by you.

BOOK XII.1

THE CAT AND THE TWO SPARROWS

To His Highness the Duke of Burgundy*

A cat and sparrow were the same in age;
from infancy their dwelling was the same;
one room contained the basket and the cage.
The little sparrow liked to play a game:
    he used his beak to tease the cat,
    who in return played pit-a-pat;
    his blows were gentle and restrained,
    just mild correction with his paws,
    and scrupulously he refrained
    from striking out with open claws.
    The sparrow was less circumspect;
    he frequently and sharply pecked.
The puss, a person of restraint and sense,
although provoked, refused to take offence,
for friends should never yield to fits of rage.
Acquainted, then, from such an early stage,
between the two, through habit, peace held sway;
their games would never turn to strife. One day
    a neighbour's sparrow came to stay;
    this new companion made a third
between the peaceful puss and flighty bird.
But then this pair of sparrows have a row,
    which Puss decides he can't allow.
'This bird presumes', he says, 'to come in here
and quarrel with my comrade just like that?
Another sparrow pick on ours? I swear
it shall not be, as I'm an honest cat.'
He joins the battle, kills and starts to eat
the neighbour's bird; then says: 'This sparrow meat
does have a most delicious taste, it's true',
and on reflection eats the other too.

To be complete, a fable, in my view,
requires a moral: these events, for me,
suggest the outline of one, which I see
obscurely still, but you, my lord, will find
quite clear at once; a simple game for you,
but for my muse a task that's hard to do;
     she and her sisters all combined
     do not possess the powers of your mind.

BOOK XII.2

THE TWO GOATS

     In nanny-goats, when they have browsed,
     a thirst for freedom is aroused,
and then they seek their fortunes. Up they go
     beyond the pastures where they graze
to solitudes that humans do not know;
and if, departing from our tracks and ways,
they find some pinnacle, or if
there is some overhanging lofty cliff,
     capriciously they strut on top:
these climbing beasts no obstacle can stop.
Two goats then, each resolving to be free,
set off on feet as white as white can be,
and left the lowly meadows lush and green
     each hoping for some happy chance.
From opposite directions they advance
towards the other one; but in between
the waters of a river intervene.
To bridge it, there is nothing but a plank.
     It isn't wide:
two weasels could not cross it side by side.
     The stream is fast, and steep the bank.

THE TWO GOATS

Our pair of amazons should quake with dread
   to see such perils just ahead,
but one of these fine ladies placed her foot
   upon the bridge; the other put
her foot on too. To me they bring to mind
the warring kings of France and Spain, no less,
when both, because a treaty must be signed,
towards each other royally progress.*
And thus across their plank, pace after pace,
these daring goats went on, till face to face
when in the middle, proudly both stood fast
   and would not let the other past.
Each had her family honour to defend,
so history says, one claiming to descend
from that fair goat of world-wide fame
that Polyphemus gave to Galatea,
the other from the nanny Amalthea,*
from whom the milk that nourished Jove once came.
   When neither of these goats withdrew
   they shared a common fate as well:
   into the water down they fell.
For those who seek their fortunes like these two
   such accidents are nothing new.

BOOK XII.4

THE OLD CAT AND THE YOUNG MOUSE

A youthful mouse, not worldly-wise,
begged mercy from a cat. He thought
that old Raminogrobis ought
to yield to reason. 'Let me live; my size',
he said, 'is small; I don't eat much; a mouse
   is not a burden on this house.

Do you believe that when I take my food
I leave our host and hostess, and their brood,
to starve? For meals I need a grain of wheat;
    a hazel-nut would make me fat.
Just now I'm thin; I'll grow, and then provide
the sort of meal your kittens like to eat.'
Thus did the captive mouse address the cat.
'You're making a mistake,' the cat replied,
    'in putting arguments to me:
you could have made a more effective plea
among the deaf. A cat, an old one too,
forgive?—that seldom comes to pass; and you
    are no exception to my laws:
    you die this moment; down you go;
    the sisters in the world below*
spin out our fates: go there and plead your cause.
As for my kittens, they'll be fed and filled
without your help.' With that, the mouse was killed.

The moral suited to my tale is plain:
the young delude themselves when they believe
that everything they want they will obtain;
    the old condemn without reprieve.

BOOK XII.5

THE AILING STAG

    Once in a place where many stags are found
        a stag fell ill; and straight away
        many a comrade hurried round,
    to visit him and help him where he lay,
    or to console at least; an irksome crowd!
        'Good sirs, just let me die in peace;

the Fatal Sisters are allowed
to settle for me, as for every one,
when I must go: so let the weeping cease.'
   But no: the comforters were bent
on proper consolation fully done,
    and in their own good time they went,
when once they'd had, to speed them on their way,
a little light refreshment—that's to say,
they all went off to graze, as was their right.
Throughout the woods nearby they chewed,
and thus destroyed the patient's store of food;
not much was left for him, scarcely a bite.
The ailing stag was now in sadder plight,
    and famine forcing him to fast,
it was from hunger that he died at last.

You doctors of the body and the soul,
to call you in exacts a heavy toll.
Oh times, oh customs!* I protest in vain:
for everyone is moved by love of gain.

BOOK XII.6

THE FOREST AND THE WOODCUTTER

A woodcutter had broken or mislaid
the handle of an axe that he had made.
The accident took time to be repaired;
meanwhile the forest and her trees were spared.
At last he humbly asked her if she would
let him remove, as gently as he could,
another branch, just one, no more,
with which his weapon might be mended.
He'd earn his daily bread elsewhere, he swore;

the forest's oaks and pinetrees, old and splendid,
revered by everyone, would not be harmed.
And in her innocence she offered aid:
the wood to make a handle for his blade.
She soon regretted it. The wretch, rearmed,
    employed the blade his handle held
to take her finest ornaments for plunder.
    She wept as each of them was felled;
by her own gift her trees were torn asunder.

Thus in our world the worldly ones behave,
applying what their benefactor gave
against himself. I weary, in these rhymes,
    of saying so; but when such crimes
    destroy our gentle woodland shade,
who would not want some protestation made?
Alas! however often I complain,
    wherever I apportion blame,
    ingratitude and wrongs remain,
    and stay in fashion just the same.

BOOK XII.16

THE ENGLISH FOX

To Madame Harvey *

Goodwill in you accompanies good sense,
with other gifts too numerous to tell:
a noble soul; ability as well
    in guiding people and events;
an open, independent disposition;
in friendship, loyalty without condition,
though Jove himself may frown, and storms arise.*
Now though these virtues should have earned

the grandest eulogy I could devise,
it would not suit the character concerned:
you don't like grandeur; praise of any sort
you find a bore. So this is plain and short.
In favour of a country loved by you,
that is, your own, I'll add a word or two.
The English are of deeply thoughtful mind;
they are by temperament that way inclined.

In every subject, as their guide
they use experiment,* and so extend
the sciences' domain on every side.
I do not say this just to please a friend:
your people lead the world in penetration.
Even your dogs* possess a keener nose
than ours in France, or any other nation.
Your foxes have more cunning. I propose,
    as proof, to tell you of a ruse,
a trick no other fox had thought to use,
a brilliant stratagem that he employed
    in order not to be destroyed.
    In dire straits, the crafty brute
—those dogs with clever noses in pursuit—
passed underneath a gallows as he fled.
There swung the creatures prone to wicked deeds,
the badgers, foxes, owls, malicious breeds,
so those who passed might notice overhead
    how they were punished for their crimes.
    At bay, their fellow-rascal climbs
to take his place among them, shamming dead.
I think of how great Hannibal misled
the Roman generals* when near defeat;
he left them baffled as he doubled back,
or sent them off along another track,
like an old fox escaping through deceit.
Beneath the gibbet where the rascal hung
    the pack arrived; its leaders checked;*
the noise was deafening; they all gave tongue.

Their master called them off, despite the din;
  how could he possibly suspect
the comic trick that saved the fox's skin?
He said: 'There is some hole he's hiding in.
The scent my dogs were after has been lost
just where these worthy persons met their end.
One day you'll come here too, my jolly friend!'
And later so he did, and to his cost.
Once more behold the foxhounds in full cry;
  behold the former corpse once more
  amongst the bodies strung up high.
  His stratagem, he had no doubt,
  would be effective, as before.
On this occasion, though, his luck ran out;
  you shouldn't use the same trick twice.
The huntsman, now, if he had had to hide,
would not have hit upon the same device.
It isn't that his brains would not suffice:
  with those, it cannot be denied,
  all Englishmen are well supplied;
it's just that living has, for them, too little charm,*
an attitude which often does them harm.
  Let me address you once again,
Madame, though not as subject for my pen.
  Prolonged expressions of esteem
are for my Muse an unrewarding theme.
  Our odes and eulogies in verse
in which the great, to flatter them, are lauded,
seldom succeed throughout the universe,
and are not much, by foreigners, applauded.
  Your monarch told you once, you say,
he'd sooner listen to a lover's song
  than eulogies four pages long.
This then is all I offer you today:
  the last endeavours of my muse,
a trifling gift; she begs you to excuse
the imperfections that these lines display.

Yet with your aid this offering of mine
might also please that lady for a while
   who brings from Aphrodite's isle
inhabitants to yours. I thus define
our duchess Mazarin,* goddess and guide
to all those Cupids living at her side.

BOOK XII.22

THE JUDGE, THE DOCTOR, AND THE HERMIT

Three saintly men once shared a common goal:
each looked to win salvation for his soul.
But 'all roads lead to Rome', and each believed
that he could choose between divergent ways,
and still attain the end to be achieved.
Compassion moved the first, because he saw
the constant worries, setbacks, and delays
entailed by cases brought to courts of law.
He offered to be arbitrator, free
of any charge.* For him, what he might earn
(this side of Heaven) was of no concern.
Man, for his sins, since laws have come to be,
determined to pursue his rights in court,
spends half his time there.—Half?—No, that's too short;
at least three-quarters; often, all his life.
Our mediator wanted, if he could,
to end this senseless and disgraceful strife.
The second saintly man, intending good,
took up a post as hospital physician,
and for this choice he earns my praise;
of all the kinds of charitable mission,
relieving illness seems to me the best.
But patients at that time were like today's:

with their demands the doctor had no rest.
Fractious and cross, they made a constant fuss.
'Of this one and of that, he takes good care—
they're friends of his; he doesn't look at us.'
You'll think that's nothing much, when you compare
the troubles that the arbitrator faced.
On neither side was anyone content:
no settlements he made were to their taste.
The scales of justice, in his hands, were bent,
they said, in favour of the other side.
The settler of disputes was sorely tried
by such remarks as these, and sadly went
        to talk things over with his friend.
Their work had brought them nothing, from the start,
but protest and complaints; they had no heart
for further effort: time to make an end.
To soothe their pain they walked past silent trees
into a wood, a place where streams ran clear
beneath high crags, untroubled by the breeze,
free from the glare of sunlight. This was where
the third of our three saints had come to dwell.
They asked for his advice. Their friend replied:
'Each man must be himself his only guide.
Who else will understand his needs so well?
To know ourselves* must be our first concern,
for thus has Majesty Divine ordained
for mortal man. As long as you remained
with others all around, what could you learn
about yourself? Such knowledge can be gained
only when living in some calmer place.
You are mistaken if you try elsewhere.
Untroubled water will reflect your face,
but look, and watch this pool as it is stirred:
what can you see?'—'What should we see, in there?
The clouds of mud have made the image blurred.'
The saint said: 'Brothers, let the waters rest,
and your reflection will again be seen.

In order to pursue the inward quest
be solitary,* tranquil, and serene.'
So spoke the hermit; and his friends agreed
to seek salvation following his lead.
   It's not that people should refrain
   from work for others; men fall ill,
they go to law, they die; they always will.
We need the doctor's care, the lawyer's brain.
But those concerned by other men's affairs
   give to their own too little weight.
Oh you who are beset by public cares,
officials, rulers, ministers of state,
who every day face conflicts and distress,
by failure crushed, corrupted by success,
only your inner self do you neglect;
like other selves, it still eludes your gaze.
And if you have a moment to reflect,
some flatterer will enter, bent on praise.
   This lesson, which will close these pages,
   is one I offer and commend
   to kings, and also to our sages.
May it be valuable in future ages!
Could I have found a better way to end?

   BOOK XII, last

EXPLANATORY NOTES

〰〰〰

Each fable has a note giving its French title and an indication of its source; further notes explain phrases or allusions which might be obscure. When notes are borrowed directly from the French editions that I have used (see the Note on Translation), the editor's name is mentioned.

SOURCES

By 'source' is meant only the origin of the narrative, and only exceptionally other elements such as dialogue. It is usually impossible to be sure which particular version of Aesop, in particular, but also of other tales, was LF's source. In such cases the source is stated simply to be Aesopic, and a reference given to the modern collection edited by Laura Gibbs (see Select Bibliography), usually without further detail, except when the particular source is probably Phaedrus (on whom see the Introduction, p. xvi). Four books of fables by him have come down to us, and are referred to here by book and number, e.g. III.7. Like those of Babrius, they can be consulted in the original, with English translation, in Perry's edition (referred to below as Perry; see Select Bibliography). The Aesopic collection that La Fontaine probably used for reference was the very full one by Isaac Nevelet (1610, republished in 1660). Among Renaissance authors, the Italians Lorenzo Bevilacqua, also known as Abstemius, and Giovanni Verdizotti, who illustrated his own fables, were also important sources for LF. Bevilacqua published 198 fables in two volumes entitled *Hecatomythia* (1495–9); they are referred to by number. For Verdizotti's fables, *Cento favole morale* (1570), there seems to be no agreed system of numbering, and I give the titles instead.

As regards another main source of LF's in the later books, the *Pañcatantra*, the ancient Indian book of statecraft expounded through animal dialogue and numerous fables, the situation is similar to that with Aesop: the work is known in very different versions in various languages. LF must have read a French version published in 1644 by Gilbert Gaulmin, the *Livre des Lumières ou la Conduite des Rois*; here the references, where possible, are to the page numbers in the translation by Patrick Olivelle (see Select Bibliography).

CLASSICAL ALLUSIONS

Many notes explain the allusions to Greek and Latin mythology, history, and institutions which LF assumed to be part of his readers' general knowledge. Nowadays some may seem daunting, but there are comparatively few areas on which he draws for poetic effect:

(i) the gods and demi-gods of Mount Olympus, though they usually have their Roman, not Greek, names: Jupiter not Zeus, Venus not Aphrodite. The main deities, and other divine or semi-divine figures such as Hercules, are not usually annotated, but there are notes on those less well-known today, such as Castor and Pollux.

(ii) the underworld, or Hades, with its rivers, notably the Styx, which the dead had to cross to reach it. Both the good and bad were there, in the Elysian Fields or (for the worst) Tartarus, as also the judges, Pluto and Minos, the three Fates (a particularly frequent allusion) who spun out the thread of human life and finally cut it, and the Furies who carried out punishments decreed by the gods.

(iii) the nine Muses, also divine, guides and inspiration in all creative arts, including history. Their abode was Mount Parnassus. In principle each covered a particular area of the arts, but the boundaries are somewhat flexible.

(iv) the Trojan war, essentially a siege, as related in the *Iliad* and *Aeneid*, of which LF does a mock-imitation in II.1. Besides the 'Trojan horse' by which Odysseus/Ulysses succeeded in entering the besieged city, the most frequent reference is the legendary reason for the war, namely the abduction of the beautiful wife of Menelaus, Helen, by the Trojan prince Paris.

(v) people, institutions, and customs, for instance Aesop and Homer, the Roman Senate, or the worship of household gods. Notes are given when the passage in question does not seem self-explanatory, as in VIII.4, when Philip of Macedon is mentioned.

THE EARLY FABLES (BOOKS I–VI)

3 *The Cricket and the Ant* (*La Cigale et la Fourmi*), I.1: source: Aesopic (Gibbs 126, *The Ant and the Cricket*). On this fable see Introduction, p. xxiv.

A cricket: traditionally female in translation, she has been, besides a cricket, a cicada, entomologically more correct for LF's 'cigale', and a grasshopper, which may be more suitable for her character. She is a cricket here because some types of cricket, as well as making a 'song', eat other insects. This circumvents the well-known criticism from the biologist J.-H. Fabre that cicadas do not do so. He has often been answered by literary critics pointing out that fable is not a realistic genre.

4 *The Fox and the Crow* (*Le Corbeau et le Renard*), I.2: source: Aesopic (Gibbs 104, *The Fox and the Raven*; Phaedrus I.13).

the Phoenix bird: the myth is that, apart from being beautiful, the bird burned to death after a cycle of hundreds of years, to be reborn from its own ashes.

The Frog who Wanted to Be as Big as an Ox (*La Grenouille qui se veut faire aussi grosse que le Boeuf*), I.3: source: Aesopic (Gibbs 349, *The Frog and the Ox*; Phaedrus I.24), and for the dialogue Horace, *Satires*, II.iii.

5 *The Two Mules* (*Les deux Mulets*), I.4: source: Aesopic (Gibbs 411, *The Two Mules*; Phaedrus II. 7).

the tax on salt: the *gabelle*, a much-hated tax under the *ancien régime*, affecting the poor more than others; the mule's pride is misplaced.

6 *The Wolf and the Dog* (*Le Loup et le Chien*), I.5: source: Aesopic (Gibbs 3, *The Wolf, the Dog and the Collar*; Phaedrus III.7). On this fable see Introduction, p. xxiv.

7 *The Heifer, the Goat, and the Sheep, in Alliance with the Lion* (*La Génisse, la Chèvre et la Brebis, en Société avec le Lion*), I.6: source: Aesopic (Gibbs 14, *The Lion, the Cow, the She-Goat, and the Sheep*; Phaedrus I.5).

8 *The Two Pouches* (*La Besace*) I.7: source: uncertain; Aesopic for the conclusion (Gibbs 527, *Jupiter and the Two Sacks*; Phaedrus IV.10).

10 *The Swallow and the Little Birds* (*L'Hirondelle et les Petits Oiseaux*), I.8: source: Aesopic (Gibbs 487, *The Swallow and the Other Birds*).

or if I stay: Couton observes that naturalists at the time were uncertain whether the swallow migrated or hid during the winter.

Those plants make snares: they are hemp, named a few lines later, from the fibres of which strong cord can be made.

11 *Cassandra . . . ignored*: this princess in Homer's *Iliad* was fated to prophesy correctly the defeat of Troy but to be disregarded.

13 *The Town Rat and the Country Rat* (*Le Rat de ville et le Rat des champs*), I.9: source: Horace, *Satires*, II.v, itself a reworking of an Aesopic fable (Gibbs 408, *The City Mouse and the Country Mouse*).

14 *The Wolf and the Lamb* (*Le Loup et l'Agneau*), I.10: source: Aesopic (Gibbs 130, *The Wolf and the Lamb*; Phaedrus I.1).

15 *The Man and his Image* (*L'Homme et son Image*), I.11: source: explained in the last lines; see next note.

M. le duc de La Rochefoucauld: a figure of great eminence because of rank, distinction in battle, and as the author of the *Maximes* (1665), a collection of brief, unsparing comments on human nature, tracing egotism or self-love in all our behaviour. See also *An Address to M. de La Rochefoucauld*, p. 172.

our new Narcissus: in Greek myth, the beautiful youth who was besotted with his own reflection in water.

16 *The Dragon with Many Heads and the Dragon with Many Tails* (*Le Dragon à plusieurs têtes, et le Dragon à plusieurs queues*), I.12: source: the anecdote is found in a miscellany, Louis Garon, *Le Chasse-ennui* (1668). The Turkish setting is no doubt camouflage for the true reference, probably the position

in the War of Devolution as between the France of Louis XIV and the Habsburg Empire (Collinet).

17   *The Thieves and the Donkey* (*Les Voleurs et l'Ane*), I.13: source: Aesopic for the story (Gibbs 62, *The Lion and the Bear*, creatures that Erasmus in his *Adages* (1508) had made into humans quarrelling over an ass). The political reference is to the situation of Transylvania in the 1660s, disputed between four powers, LF's 'thieves': a ruler of its own; Turkey; Hungary; and the Habsburg Empire.

18   *Simonides is Saved by the Gods* (*Simonide préservé par les Dieux*), I.14: source: Aesopic (Gibbs 166, *Simonides and the Twin Gods*). On this fable see Introduction, p. xxiv.

   Malherbe: much revered as a poet; see the note to p. 47, *The Miller, his Son, and the Ass*.

   Simonides: from the island of Cos, he was celebrated in the sixth to fifth centuries BC. The story is told in several ancient sources.

   Leda's sons: Zeus in the guise of a swan raped the pregnant Leda, wife of Tyndarus; the offspring, in two eggs, were Castor and Pollux, along with Helen and Clytemnestra.

20   *Olympus and Parnassus*: the mountains which were the mythical dwelling-places of gods and muses, but here code for royalty and nobility on the one hand and writers on the other.

   Death and the Unhappy Man; *Death and the Woodcutter* (*La Mort et le Malheureux*; *La Mort et le Bûcheron*), I.15 and I.16: sources: as LF explains, he invented the first, apart from the quotation from Maecenas (see below), while the second is Aesopic (Gibbs 484, *The Poor Man and Death*). On these fables see Introduction, p. xviii.

   once wrote: Maecenas was the wealthy patron especially of Horace, in the reign of Augustus. The lines are recorded by Seneca in his first *Epistle*, but are also in Montaigne's *Essais* (II.37); LF knew both.

21   *someone*: editors suggest either Boileau or Olivier Patru (see Introduction, p. xvii), who had translated into prose this fable of Aesop's.

   soldiers . . . lodged and given board: ordinary citizens could be required to do this.

22   *The Middle-Aged Man and his Two Loves* (*L'Homme entre deux âges, et ses deux Maîtresses*), I.17: source: Aesopic (Gibbs 584, *The Bald Man and His Two Mistresses*).

23   *The Fox and the Stork* (*Le Renard et la Cigogne*), I.18: source: Aesopic (Gibbs 156, *The Fox and the Stork*).

24   *The Boy and the Schoolmaster* (*L'Enfant et le Maître d'Ecole*), I.19: source: Aesopic (Gibbs 289, *The Drowning Boy*), in which the rescuer is simply a passerby. It seems likely that LF himself replaced him by a schoolmaster.

25 *The Cock and the Pearl* (*Le Coq et la Perle*), I.20: source: Aesopic (Gibbs 403, *The Rooster and the Pearl*).

26 *The Hornets and the Honey-Bees* (*Les Frelons et les Mouches à Miel*), I.21: source: Aesopic (Gibbs 178, *The Bees, the Drones and the Wasp*). LF presumably changed drones to hornets to make the legal proceedings more ridiculous.

27 *the oysters . . . shells to gnaw*: a point made more fully in IX.9, *The Oyster and its Claimants* (p. 158).

The Oak and the Reed (*Le Chêne et le Roseau*), I.22: source: Aesopic (Gibbs 202, *The Oak Tree and the Reed*), much elaborated.

28 *Against Those of Fussy Tastes* (*Contre ceux qui ont le goût difficile*), II.1: source: Phaedrus IV.7.

29 *my tales have shown . . . talking creatures*: the references are to *The Wolf and the Lamb* (I.10) and *The Oak and the Reed* (I.22), and a few lines further on to *The Fox and the Crow* (I.2).

around the Trojan wall: this sample of epic style about the Trojan war derives more from Virgil (*Aeneid*, Bk II) than from the *Iliad* itself. In Phaedrus the parody of epic style concerns the story of Medea.

down the scale: epic ranked highest among the types of poetry; what follows illustrates another style inherited from the classical world, the pastoral, complete with conventional names such as Amaryllis.

30 *The Rats who Held a Council* (*Conseil tenu par les Rats*), II.2: source: probably Bevilacqua, 197, one of many versions of the tale of 'belling the cat'.

Rodilard: a name borrowed from Rabelais's *Quart livre*; 'nibbler of bacon'.

32 *The Two Bulls and the Frog* (*Les deux Taureaux et une Grenouille*), II.4: source: Aesopic (Gibbs 12, *The Frogs and the Battle of the Bulls*; Phaedrus I.30).

33 *The Wounded Bird and the Arrow* (*L'Oiseau blessé d'une Flèche*), II.6: source: Aesopic (Gibbs 43, *The Eagle and the Arrow*).

that Prometheus bred: in Greek myth, Prometheus created the human race (LF has 'Japet', Iapetos, the father of Prometheus).

34 *The Lion and the Fly* (*Le Lion et le Moucheron*), II.9: source: Aesopic (Gibbs 243, *The Gnat and the Lion*).

35 *The Lion and the Rat*; *The Dove and the Ant* (*Le Lion et le Rat*; *La Colombe et la Fourmi*), II.11 and 12: sources: Aesopic (Gibbs 70, *The Lion and the Mouse*; Gibbs 71, *The Ant, the Pigeon and the Bird-catcher*).

38 *The Astrologer in the Well* (*L'Astrologue qui se laisse tomber dans un puits*), II.13: source: Aesopic (Gibbs 314, *The Astronomer and the Thracian Woman*, for the initial anecdote). Astrology, very influential at the time, was frequently the target of rationalist attack.

39 *and stars must influence each earthly thing*: LF preserves the old belief that stars 'influence' physical bodies, but in unknowable ways, not to be inferred from their changing positions in the sky as the astrologers claim; only God can know the future (Couton).

and puts at risk himself and his affairs: as illustrated later in the tale of Perrette (VII.9), which ends with greater sympathy for those dreaming of castles in Spain.

The Hare and the Frogs (*Le Lièvre et les Grenouilles*), II.14: source: Aesopic (Gibbs 248, *The Hares and the Frogs*), for the ending. The character-study of the hare is presumably LF's own.

41 *my eyes wide open*: the traditional belief about sleeping hares, apparently because the slightest noise awakens them and they were never seen with eyes closed (Fumaroli).

42 *The Cock and the Fox* (*Le Coq et le Renard*), II.15: source: originally Aesopic (Gibbs 149, *The Fox, the Rooster and the Dog*), often changed in adaptation, notably by Guillaume Guéroult, *Premier livre des emblèmes*, 1551, which LF probably followed (Couton).

43 *The Lion who went Hunting with the Ass* (*Le Lion et l'Ane chassant*), II.19: source: Aesopic (Gibbs 217, *The Donkey and the Lion Go Hunting*; Phaedrus I.11).

44 *Aesop's Explanation of a Will* (*Testament expliqué par Esope*), II.20: source: Aesopic (Gibbs 549, *The Mother and her Three Daughters*; Phaedrus IV.5).

45 *villas with their bars*: LF's 'maisons de bouteille', a contemporary idiom, explained by editors as houses in the country where the owners would put on drinking parties for their friends.

46 *they would no longer own the family estate*: because under ancient law the wife's assets pass into the ownership of the husband.

47 *The Miller, his Son and the Ass* (*Le Meunier, son Fils et l'Ane*), III.1: source: Racan's *Mémoires*, for Malherbe; for the story he tells, Verdizotti's first fable, *Del Padre et del figliuolo che menavan l'Asino*. It has been argued that this was the first of the *Fables*, dating from about 1647, on rather slight evidence: at that time LF's great friend Maucroix was faced with the question raised by Racan in the fable's first section: what should he do with his life? However, the fables in the early books are almost all Aesopic, whereas this one relies on Verdizotti, like two others in Book III (3 and 16), and its prologue also differs from any other. If it was indeed written before 1650 it does not seem to have had any immediate sequel.

Racan . . . Malherbe: François de Malherbe (1555–1628) imposed by example and teaching the classical form of French poetry, strictly formal, clear, and often stately; not a model often followed by LF. This fable's formality no doubt pays homage to him. Honorat de Racan (1589–1670), admired by

LF, was a favourite disciple of Malherbe's.

50 *Nicholas . . . in the song*: the song has been preserved; in it Jeanne, the girl he goes to woo on his ass, tells him to go away and not come back.

51 *The Wolf in Shepherd's Clothing* (*Le Loup devenu Berger*), III.3: source: Verdizotti, *Il Lupo e le Pecore*.

the shepherd's bagpipes too he bore: the *musette* that shepherds customarily carried was a simple form of bagpipes.

53 *The Frogs who Asked for a King* (*Les Grenouilles qui demandent un Roi*), III.4: source: Aesopic (Gibbs 27, *Jupiter and the Frogs*; Phaedrus I.2), the tale often known as King Log and King Stork.

55 *The Fox and the Goat* (*Le Renard et le Bouc*), III.5: source: Aesopic (Gibbs 113, *The Fox and the Goat*).

56 *The Gout and the Spider* (*La Goutte et l'Araignée*), III.8: source: a letter by Petrarch (1304–74), who described it as an old wives' tale; it is included in sixteenth-century collections of Aesopic fables, but it is not known where LF found it.

57 *student of Hippocrates*: a doctor.

58 *The Wolf and the Stork* (*Le Loup et la Cigogne*), III.9: source: Aesopic (Gibbs 46, *The Wolf and the Crane*).

59 *The Lion Defeated by a Man* (*Le Lion abattu par l'Homme*), III.10: source: Aesopic (Gibbs 186, *The Lion and the Man Disputing*).

The Fox and the Grapes (*Le Renard et les Raisins*), III.11: source: Aesopic (Gibbs 255, *The Fox and the Grapes*).

from Gascony . . . from Normandy: Gascons were reputed to be boastful swaggerers; Normans to speak ambiguously, 'répondre en Normand' meaning to answer without committing oneself.

60 *The Lion in Old Age* (*Le Lion devenu vieux*), III.14: source: Aesopic (Gibbs 422, *The Old Lion and the Donkey*).

The Drowned Woman (*La Femme noyée*), III.16: source: Verdizotti, *D'un Marito che cercava . . . la moglie affogata*. LF's fable, often considered misogynistic, is less clearly so than his source. J.-D. Biard, in his edition of the original plates (see under Chauveau in the Select Bibliography), notes that Chauveau's illustration, unusually, shows something that is not in the fable, namely that the woman's body is caught under a rock, downstream from where the men are talking; in other words the second speaker's remark is wrong.

61 *The Cat and an Old Rat* (*Le Chat et un vieux Rat*), III.18: source: Aesopic (Gibbs 298, *The Mice and the Weasel*, Phaedrus IV.2, and 299, *The Chickens and the Cat*).

Rodilard: he appears in II.2, *The Council of the Rats*.

64 *The Lion in Love* (*Le Lion amoureux*), IV.1: source: Aesopic (Gibbs 355, *The Lion and the Farmer's Daughter*).

Mademoiselle de Sévigné: then aged 23, the daughter of Mme de Sévigné, many of whose famous letters were addressed to her in Provence, after her marriage in 1669 to the Marquis de Grignan. As LF makes clear, she was celebrated both for her beauty and her resistance to love. Not long before the first collection of *Fables* was printed in 1668, she was rumoured to be a possible future mistress of Louis XIV (Fumaroli), which raises some questions about the figure of the lion in the fable.

66 *The Shepherd and the Sea* (*Le Berger et la Mer*), IV.2: source: Aesopic (Gibbs 275, *The Shepherd and the Sea*).

goddess of the deep: LF names her: Amphitrite, Neptune's wife.

Corydon or Tircis: names in Virgil's *Eclogues*, used ever since in pastoral poetry to denote similar characters, prosperous owner-shepherds.

68 *The Gardener and his Lord* (*Le Jardinier et son Seigneur*), IV.4: sources: nothing significant has been found. LF presumably invented the incident from what he knew of such situations in real life.

to the local lord he went: as a commoner he cannot, by law, hunt the hare, only try to frighten it away or trap it, so has to appeal to a nobleman.

70 '*Like royalty at play*': LF has 'Ce sont là jeux de prince', the beginning of a saying that the man prudently truncates. In full it continues: '. . . qui ne plaisent qu'à ceux qui les font', i.e. 'These are games for princes, which please nobody except those who play them'.

The Battle of the Weasels and the Rats (*Le Combat des Rats et des Belettes*), IV.6: source: Aesopic (Gibbs 455, *The Mice and the Weasels*; Phaedrus IV.6).

72 *The Ape and the Dolphin* (*Le Singe et le Dauphin*), IV.7: source: Aesopic (Gibbs 324, *The Monkey and the Dolphin*).

Arion: the elder Pliny, mentioned by LF a few lines earlier, tells in his *Natural History*, Bk IX.viii, the story of Arion, found originally in Herodotus. He was a famous singer; when on a voyage, the sailors plotted to throw him into the sea, in order to obtain his money. He asked for permission to sing one last song before jumping overboard; he was rescued by a dolphin who had heard the song.

74 *Piraeus*: the port of Athens, as the dolphin knows, but not the ape.

Vaugirard: now part of Paris, then a village outside the city.

The Wolf, the Nanny-Goat, and her Kid; *The Wolf, the Mother, and her Child* (*Le Loup, la Chèvre, et le Chevreau*; *Le Loup, la Mère, et l'Enfant*), IV.15 and IV.16: sources: Aesopic (Gibbs 301, *The She-Goat, the Kid, and the Wolf*, for the first; for the second, Gibbs 282, *The Wolf and the Nurse*, and 283, *The Wolf and the Nurse*).

77 *The Miser who Lost his Treasure* (*L'Avare qui a perdu son Trésor*), IV.20:
    source: Aesopic (Gibbs 407, *The Miser and his Gold*).

    Diogenes: an Athenian Cynic philosopher, he lived in the greatest self-
    denial, according to legend in a tub.

79 *The Master's Eye* (*L'Oeil du Maître*), IV.21: source: Aesopic (Gibbs 336,
    The Stag Among the Cattle; Phaedrus II.8).

80 *tears*: tradition had it that stags at bay would weep.

    The Skylark and her Young, and the Owner of a Field (*L'Alouette et ses Petits,
    avec le Maître d'un Champ*), IV.22: source: Aesopic (Gibbs 293, *The Crested
    Lark and the Farmer*, from the second-century AD writer Aulus Gellius,
    Attic Nights, II.29).

84 *The Woodcutter and Mercury* (*Le Bûcheron et Mercure*), V.1: source: Aesopic
    (Gibbs 474, *The Man, Hermes, and the Axes*).

    To M. L. C. D. B.: Monsieur le Comte de Brienne, a friend with whom LF
    collaborated on a collection of Christian poetry published in 1671.

    his aim: to instruct and entertain at the same time (as indicated a few lines later).

    as in the puny beast . . . the ant, the fly: the references are to two fables above,
    I.3, 'The Frog who Wanted to Be as Big as an Ox', and I.10, 'The Wolf and
    the Lamb', and for the ant and fly, to IV.3, *La Mouche et la Fourmi* ('The
    Fly and the Ant'), not translated here, in which the insects debate which is
    superior. The ant, portrayed more favourably than in I.1, clearly wins by
    boasting that her hard work provides food all the year round.

85 *the lesser god he sends, as go-between*: Mercury's duties as Jove's messenger
    might include taking the kind of message meant here, as in Molière's
    Amphitryon, a recent production when this fable was published in 1668.

86 *The Pot of Iron and the Pot of Clay* (*Le Pot de Fer et le Pot de Terre*), V.2:
    source: no doubt Aesopic (Gibbs 52, *The Two Pots*), but in this the two
    pots float down a river. It seems likely that LF embroidered a well-known
    passage in Ecclesiasticus, warning against 'fellowship with one that is
    mightier and richer'; the example is a kettle and an earthen pot, 'for if the
    one be smitten against the other, it shall be broken' (13:2).

87 *The Fisherman and the Little Fish* (*Le Petit Poisson et le Pêcheur*), V.3:
    source: Aesopic (Gibbs 287, *The Fisherman and the Little Fish*).

89 *The Ploughman and his Children* (*Le Laboureur et ses Enfants*), V.9: source:
    Aesopic (Gibbs 494, *The Farmer and his Sons*).

90 *The Mountain that Gave Birth* (*La Montagne qui accouche*), V.10: source:
    Aesopic (Gibbs 280, *The Mountain in Labour*; Phaedrus IV.24), and see the
    next note.

    an author: Horace, in a famous passage from the epistle *Ad Pisones*, and
    Boileau, in his *Art poétique*, III, both employed the tale as a means of

satirizing a grandiloquent author. Whether LF meant anyone in particular is not known.

92 *The Doctors* (*Les Médecins*), V.12: sources: Aesop, *The Patient and his Symptoms* (Gibbs 585) and *The Doctor and his Dead Patient* (Gibbs 587).

Nature's debt: a traditional expression in both English and French: life is a gift or loan from Nature.

The Hen that Laid the Eggs of Gold (*La Poule aux oeufs d'or*), V.13: source: Aesop, *The Man and the Golden Eggs* (Gibbs 434; she observes that other ancient sources make the magic bird a goose, as in the familiar English version).

94 *The Snake and the File* (*Le Serpent et la Lime*), V.16: source: Aesop, *The Viper and the File* (Gibbs 305).

95 *The Bear and the Two Friends* (*L'Ours et les deux Compagnons*); source: Aesop, *The Two Friends and the Bear* (Gibbs 91); but the idea of selling the skin in advance is found only later, both in the *Mémoires* of Philippe de Commines (1475), well-known in the seventeenth century, and in Bevilacqua, 49.

Dindenault: a character in Rabelais's *Quart livre*, trying with much persistence to sell sheep to Panurge.

96 *The Donkey Clad in the Skin of a Lion* (*L'Ane vêtu de la peau du Lion*), V.21: source: Aesop, *The Fox, the Donkey and the Lion Skin* (Gibbs 322) and *The Farmers, the Donkey and the Lion Skin* (Gibbs 323).

Martin-Cudgel: a character ('Martin-bâton') that LF takes from Rabelais: a servant employed as guard and armed with a big stick.

his mill: where the donkey would normally have been at work.

97 *The Shepherd and the Lion*; *The Lion and the Huntsman* (*Le Pâtre et le Lion*; *Le Lion et le Chasseur*), VI.1 and VI.2: sources: Aesopic (Gibbs 229, *The Shepherd and the Lion*, and 230, *The Hunter and the Lion*).

Another Greek . . . both elegant and terse: LF in his own note calls him Gabrias, the early author (perhaps first century AD) now named Babrius or Babrias, of whom little is known. See Gibbs, p. xxii, and for the fable, Perry, 112–13. Some of the fables now ascribed to him are indeed very brief; in the seventeenth century they had been published in quatrains. Spartans were known among other things for using few words.

99 *The Cockerel, the Cat, and the Little Mouse* (*Le Cochet, le Chat et le Souriceau*), VI.5: source: Verdizotti, *Il Topo giovine, la Gatta, e'l Galletto*.

100 *The Hare and the Tortoise* (*Le Lièvre et la Tortue*), VI.10: source: Aesopic (Gibbs 237, *The Tortoise and the Hare*).

four grains of hellebore, at least: double the traditional folk remedy for madness.

103 *The Villager and the Snake* (*Le Villageois et le Serpent*), VI.13: source: Aesopic (Gibbs 440, *The Farmer and the Frozen Viper*; Phaedrus IV.20).

104 *The Sick Lion and the Fox* (*Le Lion malade et le Renard*), VI.14: source: Aesopic (Gibbs 18, *The Fox, the Lion and the Footprints*).

105 *The Dog Who Gave Up the Substance for the Shadow* (*Le Chien qui lâche sa Proie pour l'Ombre*), VI.18: source: Aesopic (Gibbs 263, *The Dog, the Meat and the Reflection*).

The Young Widow (*La jeune Veuve*), VI.21: source: Bevilacqua, 14. On this fable see Introduction, p. xxiii.

106 *the Fount of Youth*: in medieval legend, a spring or fountain in a desert spot somewhere in the East, which had the power to restore youth.

THE LATER FABLES (BOOKS VII–XII)

108 *The Animals Sick of the Plague* (*Les Animaux malades de la Peste*), VII.1: source: probably one of the sixteenth-century fabulists, Guillaume Haudent (*Apologues*, 1547) or Guillaume Guéroult (*Emblèmes*, 1550). Versions of the fable had been used by preachers since the Middle Ages to attack abuses of the confessional, rather than flattering royal counsellors, as here (Couton, Collinet). A manuscript copy, not in LF's hand, bears the date 1674.

110 *The Man who Married Badly* (*Le Mal Marié*), VII.2: source: Aesopic (Gibbs 570, *The Man and his Ill-tempered Wife*).

112 *The Rat Who Retired from Worldly Life* (*Le Rat qui s'est retiré du Monde*), VII.3: source: none identified. Editors suggest that LF invented the rat as a parallel to a monk because, in 1675, the regular clergy refused to contribute to a tax paid by the Church to the king, which at the time was being used to fund the war against Holland. A manuscript dates the fable May 1675.

legends that Levantines tell: no doubt a disguise (see note above) for a tale of LF's own.

113 *A dervish*: another piece of disguise, part of the ironic disclaimer that the target was Christian clergy.

The Heron; The Girl (*Le Héron; La Fille*). In some editions this double fable is made into two. Sources: nothing has been certainly identified for *The Heron; The Girl* may be based on a short poem on the same topic by LF's acquaintance Conrart.

the Latin poet's fussy rat: Horace's, in his *Satires* (II.vi), imitated by LF in *The Town Rat and the Country Rat* (p. 13).

115 *She was a précieuse*: preciosity was an important feminist tendency in seventeenth-century France, a civilizing influence on the crudity of manners early in the century, but later mocked by satirists (notably Molière) for prudishness and over-refinement.

116 *The Wishes* (*Les Souhaits*), VII.5: source: uncertain. The folktale that supplies the title and the ending, usually known as 'The Three Wishes', occurs widely in very different versions, and was no doubt known in one

form or another to LF, but no accepted source has been found for the figure of the sprite, nor for the combination of Indian and Nordic elements.

118 *The Coach and the Fly* (*Le Coche et la Mouche*), VII.8: source: originally Phaedrus, III.6, embellished by memories of LF's journey by coach to Limoges (Collinet).

119 *The Milkmaid and the Can of Milk* (*La Laitière et le Pot au Lait*), VII.9: source: similar tales are widespread (see the first note below); LF's is close to a version in Bonaventure des Périers, *Nouvelles récréations et joyeux devis* (1558), XIV.

120 *The Milkmaid is its name*: Rabelais (*Gargantua*, XXXIII) mentions a fairground play on this subject, and it seems likely that LF had himself seen something of the kind.

Pyrrhus; Picrochole: both are figures ambitious for worldwide conquest, the former a great general of the third century BC, born in Epirus, the latter a character in Rabelais (*Gargantua*, XXXIII, again).

121 *The Curé and the Dead Man* (*Le Curé et le Mort*), VII.10: source: a real incident, recorded by Mme de Sévigné in a letter dated 26 February 1672. The dead man was the Comte de Boufflers.

Chouart: not the unfortunate curé's real name; LF took it from Rabelais (*Pantagruel*, 21), who gives it a sexual meaning similar to the English 'John Thomas'.

a niece of his: in French popular tradition the phrase 'la nièce du curé' signifies a woman living with him supposedly as his relative. Chouart appears to be on comparable terms with the servant.

122 *Perrette*: the heroine of the preceding fable.

The Two Cocks (*Les deux Coqs*), VII.12: source: Aesopic (Gibbs 454, *The Two Roosters and the Eagle*).

By love . . . had bled: on Troy see the prefatory notes on classical allusions above. The Scamander is a river in the Trojan plain; in Homer (*Iliad*, V), Mars and Venus were both wounded there.

123 *The Soothsayers* (*Les Devineresses*), VII.14: source: none has been identified, but fortune-tellers did a thriving trade, and in 1676 a trial of a notorious poisoner, Mme de Brinvilliers, during the course of the 'affaire des poisons', had brought them much scandalous publicity (added to a few years later by another trial, that of Catherine Deshayes, known as La Voisin). LF's satire is in line with the official campaign against such superstitious practices.

124 *if women thought . . . hard to bear*: an indirect allusion to the sale of love-potions and poisons by unscrupulous soothsayers. Mme de Sévigné, in a letter (31 January 1680) subsequent to the date of this fable, writes that LF's patron the Duchesse de Bouillon was seriously implicated in the 'affaire

des poisons', being suspected of having asked La Voisin for poison to get rid of her aged husband.

125 *The Cat, the Weasel, and the Little Rabbit* (*Le Chat, la Belette, et le petit Lapin*), VII.15: source: *Pañcatantra*, III (Olivelle 118–20, *Partridge and Hare Take their Case to the Cat*). On this fable see Introduction, p. xxx.

her household gods: like the Roman 'lares et penates'.

126 *the local rats*: because rats and weasels are enemies (as on p. 70).

127 *Death and the Dying Man* (*La Mort et le Mourant*), VIII.1: source: Bevilacqua, 99. LF also took much of Death's speech from Lucretius, *De natura rerum*, III.

129 *The Cobbler and the Financier* (*Le Savetier et le Financier*), VIII.2: sources: originally two; the shoemaker whose new-found wealth stops him singing is from Bonaventure des Périers, *Nouvelles récréations*, XXI, and the rich man's gift to a poor man from Horace, *Epistles*, I.vi. The two had apparently been combined in versions before LF's, but the incorporation into the narrative of the cobbler's problem with saints' days seems to be due to him (see note below).

Seven Wise Men: from each of seven ancient Greek cities, Solon, Thales, and others figured in a work by Plutarch, *The Banquet of the Seven Wise Men*.

131 *The trouble is saints' days*: like Sundays decreed as rest days by the Church, their number had gradually increased. Colbert sought to reduce them, for economic reasons, and succeeded against resistance in removing 17, which still left 38. The shoemaker's protests reflect government policy.

132 *The Power of Fables* (*Le Pouvoir des Fables*), VIII.4: sources: Aesopic, *Demades and the Athenians* (Gibbs 1); Plutarch, *Lives of the Orators*, VIII, tells a similar tale about Demosthenes (Gibbs 2), who like LF's orator warned the Athenians against Philip of Macedon (see note on Philip below).

Monsieur de Barillon: known to LF from Mme de Sablière's salon. He was sent as ambassador to the court of Charles II in 1677, to try to prevent the English allying themselves with Holland against France.

of Rabbit versus Weasel: see p. 125, *The Cat, the Weasel and the Little Rabbit*, VII.16.

Is it not time . . . against his every blow: Louis XIV's war against Holland, intended to be a swift campaign, had dragged on for years. Among other European powers, notably in England, where Charles II but not his nation was an ally, Louis's pan-European ambitions aroused deep suspicion and hostility.

133 *Our goddess Ceres*: although Pallas Athene was the goddess of Athens itself, Ceres (Demeter in Greek mythology) was worshipped in its region, Attica, especially at Eleusis.

134 *In Philip's war . . . the risks we run*: Philip II of Macedon (*c*.382–336 BC), the most powerful statesman and strategist of his time, father of Alexander

the Great. He was frequently the enemy of Athens in war and diplomacy. If LF meant him as a disguise for William of Orange, later William III of England, he was showing great foresight.

134 *Donkey-Skin*: in French 'Peau d'Ane', a very well-known folktale in which the heroine disguises herself in the skin of a donkey. In 1694 Charles Perrault, who knew LF well, was to publish a rhymed version of it.

Women and Secrets (*Les Femmes et le Secret*), VIII.6: source: Bevilacqua, 129.

135 *The Bear and the Gardener* (*L'Ours et l'Amateur de Jardins*), VIII.10: source: *Pañcatantra*, I; not in Olivelle.

half-licked bear: bears were a byword for ugliness in any case (as in I.7); LF's description here alludes to the medieval notion that they were born a formless lump and were literally licked into shape by the mother.

136 *Bellerophon*: a warrior hero who rode the winged horse Pegasus, but who, according to Homer (*Iliad*, VI), after suffering misfortunes wandered the world in great dejection.

Flora's priest . . . Pomona's shrine: Roman goddesses of flowers and fruit.

Gascon swagger: men from Gascony had a reputation for boastful over-confidence.

137 *The Funeral of the Lioness* (*Les Obsèques de la Lionne*), VIII.14: source: Bevilacqua, 148.

138 *men . . . are mere machines*: in Cartesian doctrine, combated by LF (see Introduction, p. xx), it is animals that are machine-like; he is using his adversary's concept as well as the fable form to degrade courtiers to animals.

so Solomon affirms: in the Book of Proverbs 20:2.

141 *The Rat and the Elephant* (*Le Rat et l'Eléphant*), VIII.15: source: Phaedrus, I.29, much modified.

the French disease: LF's readers would have known that, whereas in France venereal disease was dubbed 'the Naples disease' ('le mal de Naples'), it was 'the French disease' in Italian parlance.

142 *The Donkey and the Dog* (*L'Ane et le Chien*), VIII.17: source: Bevilacqua, 109.

143 *Jupiter and the Thunderbolts* (*Jupiter et les Tonnerres*), VIII.20: source: for the thunderbolts of different kinds, a passage in Seneca, *Quaestiones naturales*, II.41. By Jupiter is meant the French king, whom loyalists liked to see as the father of his nation. Accordingly, if the government made harsh decrees (or 'thunderbolts') it was not his doing, but the fault of his ministers—here the other, lesser gods. Couton gives literary examples of the use of this analogy.

144 *the sisters of the night*: the furies or Eumenides, as Jupiter has ordered, the agents of divine wrath. That Alecto was the fiercest seems to be poetic invention.

He who masses . . . by the Styx: the descriptive phrase is from Homer; to swear by the Styx was an unusually solemn oath, although in this case the other gods do not take it seriously.

145 *The Wolf and the Huntsman* (*Le Loup et le Chasseur*), VIII.27: source: *Pañcatantra*, II (Olivelle 84, *How the Greedy Jackal Died Eating a Bowstring*).

148 *The Unfaithful Guardian* (*Le Dépositaire infidèle*), IX.1: sources: *Pañcatantra*, I (Olivelle 66–7, *The Iron-Eating Mice*), and for the second anecdote, perhaps a fairground show, as suggested by Collinet.

Memory's nine daughters: the Muses were the daughters of Zeus and Mnemosyne.

language used by gods: verse.

149 *Solomon the Wise*: LF has *le Sage*, which would mean Solomon, traditionally the author of the Book of Proverbs, although the quotation comes from the Book of Psalms (115:11).

151 *The Two Doves* (*Les deux Pigeons*), IX.2: source: *Pañcatantra*, I; not in Olivelle. Fumaroli notes that although the characters are pigeons in the original, French 'pigeon' could then mean either a pigeon or a dove (as for the peasant in II.12). Translators differ on the point. I have followed Moore (who has 'turtle-doves') and Wood on the grounds that it seems more appropriate for the characters to be doves.

154 *Venus' son*: Cupid.

The Acorn and the Pumpkin (*Le Gland et la Citrouille*), IX.4: source: a sketch by the famous fairground comedian Tabarin, published in 1622 and later, which LF could either have read or seen performed.

155 *The Metamorphosis of the Mouse* (*La Souris Métamorphosée en Fille*), IX.7: source: *Pañcatantra*, III (Olivelle 131–3, *The Mouse that Turned into a Girl*).

156 *Pythagoras*: according to tradition, he brought back from India the doctrine of metempsychosis, the transmigration of souls from one kind of being to another.

the Grecian beauty's sake: Helen.

Boreas: a name in Greek mythology for the north wind.

157 *Lady This or Madam That*: editors cite La Grande Mademoiselle, Louis XIV's cousin by marriage, who in 1670 wished to marry the Comte de Lauzun, generally regarded as ugly.

158 *The Oyster and its Claimants* (*L'Huître et les Plaideurs*), IX.9: source: said by Boileau's biographer Brossette to come from an old Italian play; in 1670 Boileau made a version of it which now concludes his *Epître II*. On the difference between him and LF concerning the writing of fables, see Introduction, p. xix.

160 *Peter Dandy*: anglicized from Perrin Dandin, the name of judges in Rabelais's *Tiers Livre* and in Racine's *Les Plaideurs*.

   The Treasure and the Two Men (*Le Trésor et les deux Hommes*), IX.16: source: the basic anecdote goes far back, to Plato according to a life of him by Diogenes Laertius. LF might also have read a version by Guéroult, *Emblèmes*, 14–17.

162 *The Two Rats, the Fox, and the Egg* (*Les deux Rats, le Renard, et l'Oeuf*; extract from the *Discourse for Mme de La Sablière*, concluding Book IX): source: that different animals, such as marmots, used the rats' device to carry things is an observation found in various accounts by travellers of LF's own time, as well as in the elder Pliny's *Historia naturalis*, VIII, but no specific source for the anecdote told here has been found. On the *Discourse*, a long argument in verse, see Introduction, p. xx.

163 *The Man and the Snake* (*L'Homme et le Serpent*), X.1: source: *Pañcatantra*; not in Olivelle.

   ingratitude personified: as for instance in VI.13, *The Villager and the Snake*.

   when his blood . . . be bought: i.e. he would be made a sacrifice to the gods.

166 *The Tortoise and the Two Ducks* (*La Tortue et les deux Canards*), X.2: source: *Pañcatantra*, I (Olivelle 51–2, *The Turtle and the Geese*).

167 *The Fishes and the Cormorant* (*Les Poissons et le Cormoran*), X.3: source: *Pañcatantra*, not in Olivelle.

168 *bringer of good news*: in the Christian sense of evangelist. LF has the ironic *le bon apôtre* (apostle).

169 *The Wolf and the Shepherds* (*Le Loup et les Bergers*), X.5: source: for the wolf looking at the shepherds, probably Aesopic, *The Shepherds, the Lamb and the Wolf*, reported very briefly by Plutarch, *Banquet of the Seven Sages*, 13 (Gibbs 392). For the rest of the story no convincing source has been found. A twelfth-century fable by Marie de France tells of a wolf who swears off meat for Lent, but it is doubtful that LF knew her work.

   In England not a wolf is to be found: by a decree of King Edgar's in the tenth century, tribute due from Welsh princes could be paid in wolf's heads rather than money, which led to the wolves' destruction.

   mothers threaten . . . the wolf for tea: as in IV.16, *The Wolf, the Mother, and her Child*.

170 *back to the Golden Age, forgoing meat*: in the ancient poets' first age of mankind, one of perfect contentment, men had supposedly been vegetarian.

   The Two Adventurers and the Talisman (*Les deux Aventuriers et le Talisman*), X.13: source: *Pañcatantra*; not in Olivelle. The extension of the meaning of 'talisman', usually a portable charm, seems to be due to LF.

   the tasks that Hercules despatched: the twelve 'labours', imposed on him originally through the enmity of Hera towards him, Zeus having fathered him on Alkmene.

172 *Sixtus*: Sixtus V, pope 1585–90. The story goes that as candidate for the papacy he used crutches in order to appear crippled, and therefore likely to die soon if elected, but when he was elected threw them away.

An Address to M. de La Rochefoucauld (*Discours à Monsieur le duc de La Rochefoucauld*), X.14: source: this is the only fable in which LF portrays himself in a scene from real life, which must be the source both of the rabbit hunt and the village dogs. See also the first note below.

this king of animals . . . as many faults as they: the man/animal comparison which runs through the fable is probably what LF refers to in its last line, when he says that La Rochefoucauld supplied its subject. One of La Rochefoucauld's *Reflections*, not published in his lifetime but certainly known to acquaintances, entitled *Du rapport des hommes avec les animaux* ('On the relation between men and animals'), contains examples of resemblances between human behaviour and that of animals, among which figure rabbits and dogs. Couton shows that LF would have known this piece, perhaps directly from La Rochefoucauld.

174 *matter much refined*: i.e. both animal and human minds are material, not immaterial as Descartes had argued (the human soul, a Christian concept, is by definition immaterial: it is not in question here). This is part of the same anti-Cartesian argument concerning animals that LF had developed at much greater length in his 'Discourse for Madame de La Sablière' at the end of Book IX (see the extract from it, the fable 'The Two Rats, the Fox, and the Egg', p. 162).

175 *interest determines how they act*: although *amour-propre* or self-love is perhaps the main theme of La Rochefoucauld's *Maximes* (see the other fable dedicated to him, p. 15), *l'intérêt* or self-interest is a related idea of scarcely less importance.

the masters of my art: fabulists in the Aesopic tradition, as mentioned in the introduction to VI.1, p. 97.

176 *The Lion* (*Le Lion*), XI.1: source: the current political situation in Europe, Louis XIV being the lion-cub whose position had been precarious when young, but who now, probably when the Treaty of Nijmegen (1678) was being negotiated, was the powerful figure striking fear into his neighbours. The leopard may be England, since the animal figures in its coat of arms.

177 *The Dream of One who Lived in Mogul Lands* (*Le Songe d'un Habitant du Mogol*), XI.4: source: for the opening anecdote, a work of the thirteenth-century Persian poet Saadi, *Gulistan* ('The Garden of Roses'), translated (1634) by André du Ryer. The later reflections on the charms of solitude have behind them a long tradition of poetry on the theme; no specific reason is known why LF should have written them at the time (about 1677 or 1678, probably), nor why he wished then to study 'the skies'.

178 *Minos*: a figure from Greek legend, although the setting is supposedly Indian. According to one myth, he was the judge of humans in the underworld, appointed because in life, as king of Crete, he was renowned for justice.

this vizier . . . that hermit: at the time, a transparent disguise first for government ministers of genuine piety, who went on religious retreats for the good of their souls, and secondly for worldly prelates more concerned with advancement at court.

by which our customs and our lives are framed: although LF had mocked astrology in *The Astrologer* (II.13), this suggests a belief in it; perhaps the lines should be considered as poetic licence.

179 *The Danube Peasant* (*Le Paysan du Danube*), XI.7: source: a work by an old friend of LF's, François Cassandre, who inserted the story into his *Parallèles historiques*, published after this fable, in 1680, but no doubt shown to LF beforehand. The original tale of righteous protest against unjust taxation is in Antonio de Guevara, *Marco Aurelio o el Reloj de Principes*, 1529 ('Marcus Aurelius or a Clock for Princes'). Couton suggests that the fable refers by implication to the French treatment of the Dutch during the war against Holland.

Aesop and Socrates: Aesop was said to have been deformed, Socrates was famously ugly.

Marcus Aurelius . . . portrayed: the Roman emperor and philosopher (reigned AD 161–80), to whom the story of the peasant is ascribed, without foundation, in Guevara's work (see note on the source, above).

181 *praetors*: high-ranking magistrates in early Roman history, their duties later came to include governorships of provinces, and eventually became only honorary.

patrician rank: originally patricians were the highest class of Roman citizen, but the distinction fell into disuse until revived by Constantine (emperor AD 306–37) as a personal mark of honour.

182 *The Old Man and the Three Youngsters* (*Le Vieillard et les trois Jeunes Hommes*), XI.8: source: Bevilacqua, 168.

185 *Odysseus and his Companions* (*Les Compagnons d'Ulysse*), XII.1: source: on Circe, Homer (see note below), but for the main idea that animals prefer their state to that of mankind, probably a dialogue in Plutarch's *Moralia* between Odysseus and one of his men, who had been transformed by Circe into a pig.

the Duke of Burgundy: grandson of Louis XIV, son of the Dauphin, and aged 12 when this fable was published. See the Introduction, p. xxi, and the note to p. 192, *The Old Cat and the Young Mouse* (XII.5). LF also dedicated to the duke, with a lengthy epistle, the whole of what is now Book XII.

186 *the daughter of the god of day, Circe*: the first great enchantress of Western literature, she appears in the *Odyssey*, X, and frequently later, for instance in Ovid, *Metamorphoses*, XIV.

188 *men behave like wolves . . . for a word*: although the idea of men taking other men as prey goes back to Plautus, its Latin formulation, 'homo homini lupus', had been made famous by Thomas Hobbes in his *De Cive*, 1649. Here LF is no doubt referring particularly to the widespread practice of duelling, which successive French governments attempted to abolish.

189 *The Cat and the Two Sparrows (Le Chat et les deux Moineaux)*, XII.2: source: unknown.

the Duke of Burgundy: see note to the preceding fable.

190 *The Two Goats (Les deux Chèvres)*, XII.4: source: Plutarch, *Historia naturalis*, VIII.76, with a happier ending. Couton suggests that LF's dénouement was inspired by an incident in Paris, when two great ladies in carriages each refused to give way to the other in a narrow street, each claiming precedence, an issue of the highest importance in aristocratic and court society.

192 *the warring kings . . . royally progress*: the Treaty of the Pyrenees (1659), putting an end to decades of war, was formally signed by the two kings the next year on an island in the river Bidassoa.

that fair goat . . . the nanny Amalthea: Ovid tells the tale of the love of the Cyclops for the nymph Galatea in *Metamorphoses*, XIII. Amalthea was either, in different versions of the myth, a prince's daughter who fed Zeus on goat's milk, or else a goat herself.

The Old Cat and the Young Mouse (Le vieux Chat et la jeune Souris), XII.5: source: as LF explains in a preceding dedication, not translated here, the young duke had requested a fable with this title. LF took the outline of a preceding fable, V.3, *The Little Fish and the Fisherman*, and changed the characters.

193 *the sisters in the world below*: the three Fates.

The Ailing Stag (Le Cerf malade), XII.6: source: a fable found in *Kalila and Dimna*, an Oriental book of statecraft illustrated by fables derived from the *Pañcatantra* and attributed to 'Locman'. A Latin version had been published by Tanneguy Le Fèvre in 1673 and a French version by Desmay in 1677. The unhappy last lines may reflect LF's recent experience of serious illness and visits from doctors and priests.

194 *Oh times, oh customs!*: Cicero's exclamation in his first speech against Catiline.

The Forest and the Woodcutter (La Forêt et le Bûcheron), XII.16: source: Aesopic (Gibbs 40, *Zeus and the Oak Trees*), but more specifically Verdizotti, *La Selva e'l Villano*.

195 *The English Fox (Le Renard anglais)*, XII.23: source: for the anecdote, a work by Kenelm Digby on the immortality of the soul (1644), also

published in Latin, presumably known to LF through Mrs Harvey. Digby says that the incident comes from his own experience (Fumaroli).

195   *Madame Harvey*: in 1683 she accompanied her brother to Paris, where he had been the English ambassador. When in London he was an ally of Barillon, the dedicatee of *The Power of Fables* (VIII.4). Mrs Harvey was the widow of another ambassador, and a friend of the Duchesse de Bouillon, a long-standing and loyal patron of LF's.

though Jove . . . arise: i.e. despite the king's displeasure. The reference is to the Duchesse de Bouillon (see note above, and the note to p. 124), whose involvement in various scandals made her unpopular with Louis XIV.

196   *In every subject . . . experiment*: at the time English science was renowned for advances made by experimental method, associated particularly with the then-new Royal Society.

Even your dogs: English foxhounds, specially bred.

great Hannibal misled the Roman generals: when on the defensive, towards the end of his long campaign against Rome in Italy itself.

its leaders checked: i.e. would not go further, the scent having led them to the spot.

197   *living has, for them, too little charm*: England was reputed to be a country where suicide was particularly common.

198   *our duchess Mazarin*: one of the famous nieces of Cardinal Mazarin, sister to the Duchesse de Bouillon, and like her living none too respectable a life, she went to England to escape from her husband, and was there, Couton notes, much courted.

The Judge, the Doctor, and the Hermit (*Le Juge arbitre, l'Hospitalier et le Solitaire*), XII, last: source: an allegory in a work by Arnauld d'Andilly, one of the pre-eminent Jansenist family, *Les Vies des saints Pères des déserts* ('The Lives of the Holy Fathers in the Deserts'), 1647–53, which LF follows closely.

to be arbitrator, free of any charge: judges under the *ancien régime* received fees from the litigants. The cost of lawsuits, which were frequent and often long-drawn-out, was notorious, as LF remarks at the end of IX.9.

199   *To know ourselves*: an echo of the Delphic precept 'Know thyself'.

200   *be solitary*: the word would have recalled the Jansenists, noted for the 'solitaries' of Port-Royal, who lived in seclusion for the good of their souls, but were not in monastic orders.

INDEX OF ENGLISH TITLES

❦